SULA

LAVINIA DERWENT

Cover illustration by Prudence Seward
Text illustrations by Louise Annand

A Piccolo Book

PAN BOOKS LTD
LONDON AND SYDNEY

First published 1969 by Victor Gollancz Ltd
This edition published 1974 by Pan Books Ltd,
Cavaye Place, London SW10 9PG

ISBN 0 330 24172 9

© Lavinia Derwent 1969
Illustrations © Louise Annand 1969

By the same author in Piccolo

RETURN TO SULA

*Printed in Great Britain by
Richard Clay (The Chaucer Press), Ltd, Bungay, Suffolk*

CONTENTS

Chapter 1

THE GANNET ROCK

THE BOY SITTING on the rock dangled his bare feet in the water to attract the seal's attention. He knew that Whiskers would come sooner or later, grunting like an old man as he hauled himself out of the water before settling down for a snooze on the sun-warmed rock. But though the seal liked to get away from the others, playing their interminable bobbing-up-and-down games in the chill Atlantic, he had no intention of falling into a trap. The boy Magnus could be trusted, but there were other human beings on the island ready to strike him a death-blow.

'Come on, Whiskers. Hurry up! It's only me.'

The boy kicked a spray of water in the seal's direction, then took a whistle out of his pocket and began to play a tune. It was a wobbly melody, up the scales and down again. Magnus was making it up, as he had made the whistle – such as it was – out of a reed. There was little chance for him, living on so small an island, unless he made things for himself.

It was called Sula, 'the gannet rock', and indeed there were more sea-birds than humans on the stony little

7

island. They perched on the crags, circled round their nests, and screamed at each other as if taking part in a perpetual quarrel. There were not only gannets, but also guillemots, kittiwakes, fulmars, puffins, oyster-catchers, and an endless variety of gulls, all seeking sanctuary and all noisily staking their claims. It was the survival of the fittest on Sula, amongst the birds as well as the human beings.

It lay like a forgotten fragment far from the mainland and not even marked on the map. But small though it was, it was wider than the world to Magnus, who knew every stick, stone, rock, and crag on it; every stunted rowan tree, every rabbit-hole. He was familiar with the birds and seals, with the wind and the weather and the changing seasons. As for the other world that lay beyond – Scotland to the east, America to the west – he cared little about *them*, or the people who lived there. Sula was all that mattered; and people meant less to Magnus than animals.

Old Whiskers, overcoming his caution, was bulldozing his way through the water towards the rock. The boy continued his monotonous music, up the scales and down again, knowing better than to stop, or make any sudden movement that would startle the seal.

'I knew you would come,' he was saying triumphantly to himself. 'I knew it!'

He kept on playing till the seal had nosed his way out and was high – if not dry – on the rock beside him. Then the two of them settled down together like old and companionable friends who needed no conversation. Whiskers gave a grunt of satisfaction as the sun seeped through his skin; and the boy stretched out beside him, the whistle back in his pocket, sharing the animal's feeling of contentment.

This was living! Being away from people and their demands, away from Gran and her shouts: 'Mag-nus! bring in the peat!' 'Mag-nus! have you fed the pig?' 'Mag-nus! go and collect the eggs!' 'Mag-nus!'

The boy, half-asleep, lay listening to the familiar sounds of lapping waves, screaming birds, a dog barking on the hill, Gran's harsh unheeded cry: 'Mag-nus!' and nearer at hand the seal's sleepy breathing.

They were both about to drowse off when a new sound took them by surprise startling the seal from his sleepiness and the boy from his feeling of deep contentment. It was a bell – the school bell – ringing insistently to summon the island children to their lessons.

Lessons! Magnus turned his back on the sound, as if that would stop the bells. More often than not, he paid no attention to them. Why should he, at his age, go to school like an infant? He would be twelve next birthday, and already he knew all there was to know about the things that mattered to him – the sea-birds, the seals, the fishes, the wild flowers. What could old Miss Macfarlane teach him out of her dreary books about dead kings and far-off places he never wanted to see? Miss Macfarlane with her 'Now, children, I want you to sit up straight...'

Magnus sat up straight, suddenly remembering. Miss Macfarlane was no longer there! She had left yesterday with the same boat that had brought the new teacher to the island, the young man with the limp. *He* would be marking the register and finding one missing. *He* would be asking, 'Where is Magnus Macduff?'

Well, who cared? Magnus would soon get the better of *him*, with his limp and his pale face, just as he had got the better of old Miss Macfarlane. No one was going to order him, Magnus Macduff, about. Even Gran, with her cuffs and blows, had never quite conquered him. He was his own master.

There had been only one interesting thing about the new schoolmaster. He had brought a dog with him. It was a different kind of dog from those on Sula. They were tough, hard-working collies; but this was a small shivering creature, with curly hair and shaky legs. More like a toy dog than a real one. It had almost tumbled overboard off the gangway until the teacher bent down and swooped it up into his arms. Magnus would not have minded if *he* had slipped into the sea, but he would have saved the dog, even though it looked such a silly little creature.

The bells gave a last warning jangle. 'I'm not coming!' Magnus shouted inside himself. 'Not coming!'

He snuggled back into position on the rock, putting

out a friendly hand to contact his companion. But Whiskers had taken alarm at the bells and was slithering back into the sea, leaving the boy on his own.

The young man was marking the register in the little schoolroom above the harbour. It was not a difficult task, for there were only fifteen names to be called, and many of them with the same surname. They were all McLeods or Cowans or McCallums. Except one.

'Magnus Macduff!'

'Please, sir; he's not here.'

It was a girl who spoke, the one who called herself Jinty. In the register, written in old Miss Macfarlane's precise hand, she was called Janet Cowan, but the whole class seemed to have other names. 'By-names', they called them. There was Red Sandy and Black Sandy, and Mirren whose real name was Mary-Ann; and Kirsty who was Kristine. There was Angus Alastair McCallum, the smallest of the lot, whom everyone called Tair. And another known as the Ferret. But the missing boy – Magnus Macduff – seemed to have no by-name.

Jinty, with the long pigtails, had volunteered the information: 'He's not here.'

'So I see,' said the teacher wearily, then pulled himself up. Weary already, and the day not begun! He was a weakling all right. But the journey yesterday and the settling-in to a new home had sapped what little energy he had. His leg was hurting, and every bone in his body ached. Perhaps his mother was right. Lady Rose Murray was seldom wrong.

'You're not ready for work yet. Andrew dear, after such a dreadful illness. It was touch and go, you know. My poor boy, *you*, of all people, to take polio. And

12

though you've made such a wonderful recovery, you've still got to take care.'

Andrew Murray was tired of taking care, tired of being called 'my poor boy', tired of being looked on with pity. He was a man, wasn't he? and he wanted to lead a man's life. Surely he could start to live again, once he was away from the cloying atmosphere of home. Away on an island with the enchanting name of Sula. He was longing to study and photograph the birds, perhaps write a book about them, and, best of all, grow strong and straight again.

'It'll be an easy job; only a few children to teach; and what could be healthier than living on an island?' he had protested. Dr Barclay had backed him up, and together they had broken down Lady Rose's objections.

'You'll be back home in a month,' she predicted. 'My poor boy, who's going to look after you?'

'Really, mother! I'm not helpless. I can get Mrs Somebody from one of the cottages...'

'It all sounds so primitive.'

'That's what I like about it,' said Andrew doggedly.

'The very thing he needs,' said Dr Barclay, supporting him.

'But he'll be so *lonely*.'

'Not I!' Lonely? All he longed for was peace.

'I tell you what, you can have Trix,' said Lady Rose, as if that settled everything.

'Oh, mother! A poodle on a place like Sula?'

'Why not? She's such a friendly little soul. She'll be good company for you.'

'Yes, I daresay, but...'

'And I really have too many dogs. I could spare Trix,' said his mother generously.

True enough, Lady Rose always had too much of everything. A clutter of dogs, all poodles, swarmed around the house. They were attractive little creatures, but not – in Andrew's estimation – *dogs*. He would have liked a sturdy spaniel or a terrier, but the poodles, and particularly Trix, the smallest of the lot, were only play-things. What would the islanders think of him, arriving with such a pet?

Just then a small white ball uncurled herself from a cushion and gazed at him with beseeching eyes.

'All right,' he sighed, reaching down and lifting the puppy into his arms. 'I'll take Trix.'

Jinty Cowan was watching the teacher with wide, un-blinking eyes. They were all watching him, for it was sel-dom they saw a new face on Sula; all except the Ferret who was guddling with a piece of blotting-paper in the inkwell in front of him. It was a pleasant pastime, one in which he had often indulged in old Miss Macfarlane's day. *She* was too short-sighted to notice what went on in front of her face; and besides, he could always take refuge behind Black Sandy's broad back. When he had made enough inky pellets, he could flick them in all directions, hitting the girls on the face or shoving them down Black Sandy's back. It was quite a good game.

'Where is he?' the new teacher was speaking to Jinty. 'Why is he not here? Is he ill?'

'Ill! Oh no!' Imagine Magnus Macduff being *ill*!

'Then why isn't he at school?'

There was a question! Even Jinty, usually so ready with her tongue, had no answer.

The new teacher was frowning at the register. 'He

14

seems to have been absent a great deal. Why? Surely someone knows the reason. Where is he?'

'Well...' began Jinty, and then stopped. He could be anywhere. Up on the crags looking for birds' eggs, maybe. Or away out on the Heathery Hill cutting peat. Or scrabbling about in the rocky pools. Or chasing Gran's cow. Or – goodness knew where.

'He's somewhere.' That was all Jinty could tell.

The teacher tried hard to swallow a feeling of irritation. Then all of a sudden he remembered catching a glimpse the day before of a sun-tanned, bare-footed boy, leaping lightly from rock to rock, coming closer to watch him as he limped off the boat. The boy had given him a bold, almost insolent stare; and he – Andrew Murray – had suddenly felt more conscious of his dragging leg, his thin body, and his pale face.

Their eyes met. There was no pity in the boy's glance – that, at least, was something. What was there instead?

15

Scorn? Or merely curiosity? Whatever it was, it had made Andrew feel uncomfortable.

The boy was not in the classroom. So it was Magnus Macduff! Andrew tightened his lips, seeing trouble ahead. It would not be easy to tame such a wild young rebel; but tamed he must be.

'Go and fetch him!'

The class sat up. Even the Ferret stopped making his inky ammunition and stared at the teacher. Fetch Magnus!

'B-But how?' asked Jinty, the spokeswoman.

'How? Just go and tell him I want to see him. Go on, one of you! You, Janet – Jinty, or whatever you call yourself. And don't come back without him! Now then; let's start our lessons.'

Jinty got to her feet uncertainly, not knowing what else to do or say. There was something about the new teacher that must be obeyed. All the same, he little knew what he was asking. Let *him* try to fetch Magnus, and he would soon find out.

As she crossed the classroom, one of the Ferret's pellets hit her smack on the cheek, but she scarcely noticed it. Absorbed in her problem, she opened the door and almost tumbled over a white curly ball sitting shivering on the doorstep, wailing like a child.

She stared at it, wondering what to do. Then suddenly she picked it up and poked her head back into the classroom. 'Please, sir, here's your wee dog.'

The teacher turned from the blackboard, while the dog tried to jump from Jinty's arms into his. The class, which had newly settled down, began to rustle again with excitement. Trix's wails gave way to joyful yelps as Andrew Murray took her and set her down by his desk.

'Stay there and behave yourself,' he said, trying to sound stern. 'Thank you, Jinty. Off you go.'

More reluctant than ever, now that there was an added attraction in the schoolroom, Jinty gave a martyred sigh and went off on her mission.

'I'm not coming!'

It was all happening as Jinty had foreseen; the scramble over the rocks to find the truant, his pretending not to see her, and his downright refusal to listen to what she had to say.

'But the teacher says...'

'He can say away,' scoffed Magnus, kicking the water. Then, pretending not to care, he asked, 'What's he like?'

Jinty considered. "He's not a bit like Miss Macfarlane.'

'Huh!'

'He's got a wee dog.'

Magnus sat up and Jinty suddenly saw how she could win.

'He's let it into the school. It's the funniest wee ...'

'I know!' Magnus wasn't going to be told about the dog by Jinty Cowan. He wasn't going to be told anything by a mere lassie. He wanted to find out for himself.

With a lithe movement he sprang up from the rock and shook the water from his bare legs.

'Are you – are you coming, Magnus?' Jinty was almost afraid to put it into words.

But Magnus would not commit himself. 'Maybe I will,' he shouted, springing from rock to rock. 'And maybe I won't.'

Jinty turned away, knowing that she had scored a victory, or, at least, that the little dog had won. She went slowly back up the steep pathway towards the school, knowing better than to expect Magnus to walk beside her. She had enough sense not to turn round to see if he was following. One false move would put him off.

He was following all right, zig-zagging up the hill as if trying to put her off the scent. She pretended not to notice that he was close behind her when she opened the schoolroom door.

'He's here!' she said in a loud whisper to the teacher, busy at the blackboard.

'Thank you, Jinty. Go to your seat. And you, too, Magnus,' he said, as the boy came sidling in. 'I'll talk to you later.'

Magnus looked him full in the face. Again that stare! Insolent? Scornful? 'Go to your seat,' repeated the teacher, in a firmer voice, prepared to stare him out. But the boy was no longer looking at him. He had fixed his gaze on the little white dog, lying asleep under the desk; and the expression on his face was no longer scornful.

Chapter 2

THE BATTLE BEGINS

I have a little shadow that goes in and out with me,
And what can be the use of it is more than I can see.

ANGUS ALASTAIR MCCALLUM, known as Tair, was saying his poetry in a sing-song voice, as he had said it a hundred times to old Miss Macfarlane. *She* had always given him a kind smile at the end and said, 'Very nice, dear. Sit down! Next please.' But the new teacher was reacting quite differently.

He had a peculiar look on his face – a mixture of amusement and annoyance. 'Must you repeat it like that?' he asked impatiently. 'What's it all about, anyway?'

Tair blinked his eyes in surprise. 'Please, sir, I don't know, sir.'

Tair had never bothered to think about it. He had just repeated it like a parrot, to please old Miss Macfarlane. But the new teacher was not so easily pleased. As for what it was all about, he must ask Avizandum. *He* would know. Avizandum knew everything.

Avizandum was Tair's best friend – his 'familiar' –

19

who lived in his pocket and was more real to him than
everybody in Sula put together. No one else believed in
his existence, but *they* were all wrong. Tair could hear
him whispering right now, 'I wish old Miss Macfarlane
was back.'

'Me, too,' said Tair out loud.

'What was that?' said the teacher, looking at him
through lowered brows.

'N-Nothing,' said Tair, while Avizandum whispered a
warning: 'Watch it!'

Magnus Macduff, sitting beside him, scribbling with
his pencil, made a sudden sound, something between a
snigger and a snort.

Andrew Murray gave him a sharp look and said, 'Sit
up, boy!' He rapped it out so suddenly that Magnus,
against his will, sat up. But the moment the teacher's eye
was off him, he slouched back again and resumed his
doodling. Who did Mr Andrew Murray think he was?

Tair was not the only one who was wishing old Miss
Macfarlane back. The whole fifteen were sitting up and
taking more notice than usual. Even the Ferret had been
forced to clear away his ammunition and get to grips
with his reading-book – a tattered inky object, which
looked as if it had come through many a battle, as indeed
it had.

They were all at different ages and stages. It was like
teaching fifteen classes instead of one, thought Andrew
Murray, dragging himself wearily from desk to desk. The
girls were brightest, and especially Jinty Cowan. It was
obvious that the boys had found old Miss Macfarlane
easy game.

The moment inevitably came when Andrew Murray's

battle with Magnus began. Like two dogs about to embark on a fight, they eyed each other up and down.

'Well?' began Andrew, opening the contest. 'What about you, Magnus Macduff?'

Magnus made no reply. What about him, indeed!

'May I see your books, please?'

Magnus's books were in little better condition than the Ferret's. Splashed with ink, torn, scribbled over with pencil, they had obviously been given rough treatment. But there was one surprising thing about them. Andrew Murray's eyes opened wide when he saw that the scribbles were more than mere doodles. There were drawings – wonderfully imaginative pictures of seals, birds, dogs – correct in every detail of anatomy, and so fresh and life-like that the creatures seemed to be crawling across the arithmetic book, and the birds flying in and out of the sums.

Andrew made no remark about the state of the books. 'You like drawing?' he asked the boy, sitting gloomily at his desk.

'Uh-huh.'

'Uh-huh? What does that mean?' said Andrew, his irritation rising.

Magnus scowled at him. What else would Uh-huh mean except Uh-huh?

The teacher decided to let it pass. 'Show me your drawing-book, please.'

'Haven't got one!'

'What? You mean you never had any drawing-lessons?'

'Uh-huh.'

Magnus said it deliberately, knowing he was annoying the pale young man. So what? The pale young man was annoying him with his silly questions. How could anyone teach him something he knew by instinct? Old Miss Macfarlane? Not likely! *She* had never clambered over the rocks and held a gull in her hand to find the length of its beak, or how one feather interweaved with another, or how its eyes opened and closed. How could *she* know what a seal looked like at close quarters, or a lamb when it was newly-born? These things had to be studied, and not in books.

'Goodness gracious!' It was all Andrew Murray could think of saying. Just in time he stopped himself from suggesting, 'I must see about giving you some lessons.' What could *he* teach this tousle-headed rebel about drawing? Certainly he had taken an all-round training as a teacher, which included a smattering of everything; but his knowledge of art was negligible. He had tried himself, and failed, to bring pictures to life. He had no feeling for it, no instinct as this boy obviously had. In the end he had torn up his few stiff sketches and taken to a camera instead. A fine one *he* was to think about teaching art to anyone, far less to this natural genius.

In an effort to re-establish his authority, he said sharply, 'Show me your reading-book!'

Magnus's reading-book was the most tattered of all – a sign, no doubt, that this was the subject he hated most. Two things about it surprised Andrew Murray as he opened it. First, there was a fresh drawing on the contents page. It was a picture of a small white dog, curled up into a sleeping ball. Trix, immortalized by Magnus Macduff's scrubby pencil. Immortalized in such a way that Andrew longed to tear out the page and keep the drawing for himself. But the second surprise was now claiming his attention.

'Surely you're beyond *that*!' he said, pointing to a picture of Henny-Penny about to set off on her adventures, with a shopping-basket under her wing, and with far finer illustrations by Magnus in the margins. 'Stand up and let me hear you read.'

Magnus flushed. He hated reading about Henny-Penny and her silly adventures. And, simple though the words were, he was still not too sure of some of them.

He shuffled in his seat, reluctant to get up. 'Come on,' said Andrew Murray impatiently. 'I'm waiting.'

The boy gave him one of his looks, and stood up. Then he began to read in a lifeless voice, stumbling over the words, while Jinty, from her desk behind, prompted him in a loud whisper. It was such a deplorable perform-ance – even Tair could have acquitted himself better – that Andrew was torn between pity and anger – pity at the boy's obvious discomfort, and anger at the thought of those missing marks on the register. A boy of Magnus's age faltering over simple words, like a baby!

'That's enough,' he said suddenly, releasing the boy from his penance. 'Stay behind after the others have gone.'

Magnus slouched back into his seat, relieved that the ordeal was over, yet furious at the teacher for finding out his weakness, and at the thought of staying behind. Miss Macfarlane had known better than to order him about like that. But give him time. There were ways in which he could conquer the new teacher.

For the rest of the day Magnus slouched in his seat, doodling absently on his book about Henny-Penny, pay-ing no attention to what was going on around him. He drew old Whiskers lying on the rock; he did another pic-ture of the little white dog standing on its hindlegs. Then with hatred in his heart he tried a caricature of the new teacher. But it was no good. Human beings escaped him. It was only when drawing animals or birds that his pencil seemed to move by itself, with sure, confident strokes.

He managed at last to get a half-likeness of his subject by drawing Bilko – old Cowan's goat – and putting Andrew Murray's pallid face on it. The goat was good, almost life-like, but he had spoilt it by trying to capture that weary look on the young teacher's face.

Suddenly he realized that the others were on their feet, ready to leave. Springing up, he tried to slink out with them; but at the door Andrew Murray called him back.

'Magnus! One moment, please! Did I not tell you to stay behind?'

'Uh-huh.'

Again that insolent look. Andrew Murray tightened his lips, trying to keep himself under control. His face was paler by now, his limp more pronounced as he crossed to his desk and picked up a book.

'I think this would be more interesting for you to read,' he said, holding it out to the boy. '*Treasure Island*. Do you know the story?'

Magnus gave a slight shake of his head, but showed no sign of interest. He took hold of the book, but did not look at it.

'Take it home, if you like,' said Andrew, trying hard to get a friendly note into his voice. 'Perhaps you would like to show it to your parents?'

Too late – by the look on Magnus's face – he realized his mistake. How stupid of him to take it for granted that the boy's parents were alive! Perhaps he had no one at home to care for him. Perhaps that was the reason for his strange behaviour. Could it be that he was unwanted, unsure of himself, clinging to his devil-may-care air to hide the fact that he was nobody's child?

'I'm sorry,' he began, feeling at a disadvantage; but the boy had moved away from him and was pitching the book carelessly on to his desk, beside the other tattered volumes, showing as plainly as he could that he cared as little for it as for them. 'Can I go now?' he said, turning round and looking at the door instead of the teacher.

'I suppose so.' Andrew Murray was too tired to fight. 'I'll see you tomorrow. Remember, Magnus, no more playing truant. You have a lot of lost time to make up. Are you listening?'

'Uh-huh.'

Magnus said it deliberately, as if bent on antagonizing the teacher. But Andrew had suddenly lost interest in him. He was searching under the desks, in the cupboard and behind the blackboard. 'Trix! Where are you?' he called in a worried voice. 'Come on! Stop hiding! Trix!'

The boy, half-way out of the door, let him search. Then suddenly he spoke up.

'She's not here. She's away.'

She was away all right! At the general exodus, Trix had got up from under her master's desk and followed at the heels of the children, thinking that *he* was coming too. She had been inactive long enough. It would be fun to get outside and be free to frisk about in the fresh air.

For a time she followed the children happily, jumping and dancing at their feet. Then as they gathered speed and ran down the steep path to the houses at the harbour, she hesitated and looked back. No sign of the familiar long legs of her master. Where was he? Should she go back and look for him?

It was then that the Ferret picked up a handful of loose pebbles to toss into the water. Catching sight of the small dog, he threw one at her instead, more in fun than in earnest. It missed, but flew near enough to startle Trix into yelping with fright, and to give the Ferret the idea that this was a better game than flipping inky blotting-paper round the schoolroom. As the dog ran off, he threw stone after stone till his hand was empty.

It was the last one that hit Trix on the leg, but she was too overcome with terror to notice it. She only knew that it was suddenly more difficult to run, and that – though the bombardment had stopped – another and more terri-fying enemy was coming towards her.

It was Bilko, old Cowan's goat, a harmless enough creature – but not in Trix's sight. To her he seemed like a bearded monster with fearsome horns, coming at her head-down, as if bent on tossing her sky-high. Where was she to turn? She could only run this way and that, limping and yelping, hoping that somehow a miracle would happen.

The miracle materialized in the form of Mangus Mac-duff, who swept her up into his arms and spoke soothing words to her, while Bilko turned tail and wandered harm-lessly away. The Ferret, fearing retribution, took off at a faster pace, and disappeared into the farthest away cot-tage where he lived. But Magnus had seen him, and tightened his lips at the sight of the blood staining the dog's leg. The Ferret could hide, if he liked. He would get his deserts later. Meantime, the dog must be com-forted and taken back to her master.

Trix shivered in his arms, and then snuggled against him, realizing that she had found a refuge. 'You'll be all right, little thing,' Magnus assured her, and carried her

26

carefully back up the hill towards the schoolhouse.

'Thank goodness! You've found her!'

There was a note of relief in the young teacher's voice as he came hurrying to meet them; but his expression changed when he saw the blood.

'Who did it? Who hurt her?' he said sharply. 'Was it you?'

Magnus did not speak. He looked at the teacher instead – a look that almost hit Andrew Murray in the face. The young man coloured. Another blunder! He might have known that a boy like Magnus, with his deep understanding of animals, could never hurt any helpless creature.

'I'm sorry...' he began. Apologizing again! Why was it that Magnus always seemed to put him on the wrong foot? 'Then who did it?' he demanded, pulling himself up.

'Don't know,' said Magnus gruffly, and handed the dog over, as if that was the end of the matter.

'But surely you must have seen...' began Andrew, and then stopped. He could tell by the look on the boy's face that he knew; but something warned him it would be best to say no more. If justice was to be done, Magnus would see to it himself.

'All right. Thank you for what you've done. Good-night, Magnus!'

The boy made no response, but gave a last look at the dog, and then turned abruptly and ran home.

Chapter 3

LEARNING A LESSON

HOME WAS A cottage in the middle of a cluster near the harbour, white-washed like the others, but different in one respect. There were no curtains at the window. Gran did not hold with fancy trimmings. Instead, there was a sturdy-looking aspidistra in a brass pot. Not that Gran held with flowers either; but the aspidistra was different. Like herself, it had survived time and storm, never needed coddling, and had no nonsense about it. It was the first thing Magnus ever remembered seeing, and now it was so familiar that he seldom noticed it at all, except when Gran shouted to him in rainy weather, 'Mag-nus! Take the aspidistra out for a drink.'

Everything in the cottage – apart from the aspidistra – was useful. There were pots, pans, and dishes on the shelves. No ornaments. No cushions on the upright chairs. No pictures on the walls. Only a grim-looking calendar advertising sheep-dip. No rugs on the stone-flagged floor. No radio. No magazines or books lying about. Everything was as plain as porridge – and Gran plainest of all.

No one knew how old she was. Perhaps not even Gran

herself. She seemed to be ageless. Certainly she was tireless. Spare and strong, with a wrinkled, weather-beaten face and sinewy arms, she could outclass any of the islanders in endurance. From early morning till dark she was out and about, with stout boots on her feet, a man's bonnet on her head, and an old coat tied round the middle with string. In wet weather she threw a sack over her head and ignored the climate.

Though Gran's croft was so small, there were neverending tasks to do – the sheep to tend, the cow to milk, the hens to feed, the peat to cut, the potatoes to gather. Butter and cheese had to be made, and scones and bread baked. Extra chores, too; for Gran helped to launch boats, gut fish, mend fences, repair broken ploughs, and was the first to turn out on a stormy night when the rocket sounded. What would Sula have done without Gran? She was the island's backbone.

Even at night when the lamp was lit Gran seldom sat down, and then only to pick up her knitting or mending. No leaning back and resting. Rest meant waste, and Gran never wasted anything, not the smallest scrap of string, nor an idle word. Yet she knew everything that went on in the island. Sometimes Magnus had an uncomfortable feeling that she even knew what he was thinking.

If he sat down for a moment to scribble his drawings on an odd piece of paper, she would be after him like a tiger. 'Mag-nus! Have you nothing better to do? What about the weeds in the garden? And the hens? Have you shut them in for the night? Mag-nus! Go and *do* something! Stop wasting your time!'

Gran always spoke to him in commands. They had no other conversation. No soft words passed between them. 'Dears' and 'darlings' were seldom heard on Sula, and never in Gran's cottage. If she was fond of the boy, she never showed it. She treated him as impersonally as she did the aspidistra.

As for his parents, Magnus knew little about them, except that his father had foundered in a fishing-boat long ago in a storm off Sula Point. His mother had died soon afterwards – of a broken heart, it was said. But what they were like, Magnus never knew. There were no photographs of them in the cottage, nothing to make them live in the boy's imagination. Only a little box covered with shells, with a watch inside, which Gran kept hidden in the dresser drawer. The box, Magnus thought, might have been his mother's, and the watch, of course, belonged to his father. Perhaps the day would come when it would be his. But Gran never spoke of it, nor mentioned his dead parents.

She was pouring some milk from a jug into a little can when Magnus came in.

'Take this!' she said to the boy, without looking at him.

'Where?'

'To the schoolmaster.'

31

Magnus's lips tightened. He had had enough of the schoolmaster; but there was no going against Gran.

'What have I to say?' he asked sulkily.

'Say? Tell him he can have the milk every day, and butter and cheese, if he wants. Tell him if he needs somebody to clean the schoolhouse, I can come for an hour in the morning, and an hour in the afternoon.'

'Oh Gran!' Surely there was somebody else on the island who could clean the schoolhouse. The less he had to do with the pale young schoolmaster the better. But Gran's word was law.

'Go on, now! And be sure to bring back the can.'

Magnus went out carrying the can in his unwilling hand. Two doors away he saw a pig-tailed figure standing waiting. Jinty Cowan! She had a habit of lurking there, waiting to waylay him as he came by. Usually he dodged off in the other direction, but today he saw his chance.

'You can do a job for me, if you like,' he said casually. Never let it be said he was *asking* for favours.

'Oh yes, I will, Magnus!' Jinty's heart was racing with excitement. 'Anything!'

Briefly he explained what she had to do. Take the milk to the schoolhouse. Give Gran's message, and remember to bring back the can.

'Oh yes, I will, Magnus!' She would have crossed the world barefoot to please him. 'Will you be here when I come back?'

'I might.'

He had a job to do first – a man's job. He had to deal with the Ferret.

Jinty waited to see if her lord and master had anything else to say. No! She could tell by the withdrawn look on

32

his face that the conversation was at an end.

'Okay, then,' she said, picking up the can of milk. 'I'm away.'

Magnus stood looking after her, but not seeing her. Like the aspidistra, she was so familiar that he hardly ever noticed her. He was too busy wondering what to do with the Ferret. Hoping, too, that Gran would not come out and find him standing at the Cowans' door instead of making his way up to the schoolhouse.

Though it was in the same row, Jinty Cowan's cottage was different from the others. Above the door in faded letters were the words POST OFFICE AND GENERAL STORE, and outside stood a bright red telephone-box. It was seldom used, except in an emergency, but it could link Sula with the whole world. Even America.

In the window there was a higgledy-piggledy clutter of tinned food, bottled sweets, brushes, toothpaste, soap, pipes, string, pans and teapots. The shop and the post office were all in one room, the shelves piled up untidily with tins, wool, boots, scrubbing-brushes, hammers, nails, hairpins, and school jotters.

The Cowans had a sitting-room, too, equally crowded, with a three-piece suite, a radiogram, chairs, cushions, footstools, and a mantelpiece full of ornaments – china dogs and cats, ships-in-bottles, and a vase full of artificial flowers.

The Cowans always seemed to have plenty of everything. They were for ever opening tins or helping themselves from the shelves in the shop. *They* seldom lived on plain fare, and Jinty was never without a bag of sweets in her pocket – sometimes even a bar of chocolate. All the same, Magnus rarely went into their house. Everything was too cloying. The fire was too hot. There were too many gee-gaws around; too much rich food on the table; too much talk-talk-talk. He preferred the open spaces, and the company of old Whiskers, the seal.

A movement from the end cottage! The Ferret was coming out, warily, watching to see if the coast was clear. Magnus slipped hastily back into the shadows of the Cowans' doorway, and got ready to pounce. The Ferret, sure of himself now, came strutting up the road, his catapult in his hand. He was off to put in some practice on old Cowan's goat – or anything else he could find for a target.

'Hi, you!' called Magnus.

Too late the Ferret saw the figure lurking in the doorway and started to run, but who could outdistance Magnus Macduff? He had hardly reached the harbour before he was tripped up. Biting, scratching, grunting – no rules to the game – the two boys fought it out, as they had fought many a battle in the past, neither of them asking nor expecting any quarter.

Sometimes Magnus was on top, sometimes the Ferret. In a way, they enjoyed the excitement of it, the feeling of fun mixed up with danger. But today it was more than a game. Magnus's thumps were harder, his determination to win stronger. He wanted to hurt the Ferret as *he* had hurt the little dog.

Finally he succeeded in wresting the catapult from the

Ferret's closed fist. He had got what he wanted!

'That's mine! Give it back! I hate you!' panted the Ferret, kicking out at him.

'No fears!' Magnus thrust the catapult into his pocket beside his own tin whistle, and got up, standing victoriously over his fallen victim. 'You're not getting it back, not after what you did, you cruel beast!'

'I never meant to hurt the wee dog,' said the Ferret, on the verge of tears. What was he going to do in the schoolroom tomorrow without his catapult? It would take ages to make a new one. 'Come on, Magnus! Give it back!'

'No!'

Magnus's No meant No. It was definite and final. The Ferret had lost the fight and he knew it. There was nothing else to do but accept the situation. He would get his own back tomorrow or the next day.

Magnus went off, fingering the catapult in his pocket. He had no intention of keeping it. There was an unwritten law of right and wrong on the island. He would give it back to the Ferret in the morning. Meantime he might as well put in a bit of practice with it himself.

He looked around for a target. A seagull came swooping down to land on the harbour wall. No, not that. Magnus studied the bird's wing-span; its feet as it landed; the way it twisted its neck round to peck at its tail-feathers. The boy's fingers were itching – not for a catapult, but for a pencil. He made a mental note of the picture he would draw in the margin of one of his lesson-books tomorrow.

The thought of lessons brought a frown to his brow. A sudden idea came into his head when he caught sight of Jinty running home with the empty can, her mission over, her face full of importance. *She* would do for a target, and not only for the catapult.

Magnus fitted in a small pebble and let fly. Ping! Straight to his objective, hitting Jinty on the bare leg.

'Ow!' Jinty jumped into the air. 'I'll murder you!' she screamed, thinking it was the Ferret up to his tricks. But when she saw that it was Magnus, her face broke into a smile. This was her day! He was fairly showing attention to her, for a change. It was an honour to be hit on the leg by *him*!

'I've done it, Magnus. Here's the can,' she said, running breathlessly towards him. 'The teacher says he'd like your Gran to come and could she start tomorrow, and he wants the milk every day and he'd like some butter and eggs, and the wee dog's got a bandage on its leg...'

'Okay! Okay!' said Magnus, stemming the flow; too lordly to say thank you, but meaning it all the same. He took the empty can and dumped it at Gran's door. Then came the difficult part. He wanted another favour from Jinty, but he was not going to ask it outright.

The long and short of it was, he was determined to learn to read properly. Not for the love of reading itself, nor for the love of the schoolmaster, but because he was not going to risk any more shame-making scenes and sarcastic remarks. He had never bothered his head in old Miss Macfarlane's day, but now he would bother, just so that Mr Clever Murray would have no cause to make a fool of him. He began to regret having left that book behind – the one about Treasure Island.

Jinty had no idea what was going on in the boy's head, but she paved the way by asking – not with much hope, 'Are you coming in?'

'I might.' He was not going to say Yes right away, nor was he going to look straight at her. 'I'll see,' he said, kicking his feet.

Jinty's face flushed. This was a great day for her, right enough! But she had better be careful about her next move.

'I'm away in, then. I'll maybe see you, Magnus.'

'Maybe.'

First of all he had a look at the sky. A good night for the fishermen, out beyond Sula Point in their boats. Then he saw a small lone figure walking by himself, and yet not alone. It was Tair talking to Avizandum. As he came nearer Magnus could hear the conversation, or at least, one side of it. Tair was asking Avizandum about the teacher's dog.

'D'you think it'll be lame all its life, like *him*? No? Oh, that's good. I wonder if it'll be in the school tomorrow? Oh, will it? That's nice . . .'

Avizandum evidently issued a warning at this point, for Tair whipped round just in time to avoid being tripped up by a stealthy figure slinking behind him. The Ferret, looking for prey.

'Watch it, you!' shouted Magnus, as Tair took to his heels and fled into the cottage where he lived. The Ferret, too, made off in a hurry, dodging round the corner out of sight. He had enough sense not to risk a second battle tonight with Magnus Macduff.

Chapter 4

TAMING THE REBEL

Jinty's reading book lay on the table, propped up against a pot of strawberry jam. She was chewing a chocolate-caramel when Magnus came in, trying to look as if he were somewhere else.

The heat of the cluttered sitting-room hit him in the face. He tripped over a footstool and sat down on a peach-coloured cushion on the sofa sooner than he had expected. With an impatient gesture he reached under him and tossed the cushion aside.

'Have a caramel,' offered Jinty, passing a paper bag towards him. There was a glint of triumph in her eye.

'No, thanks,' he said gruffly. He had come for a purpose and it was not to sit on peach-coloured cushions stuffing himself with chocolate-caramels. 'Er – are you doing your lessons?'

'It doesn't matter,' said Jinty, hastily closing the book, ready and willing to be at his service. But to her surprise he took the book from her and opened it at the first page. It was called *Tom and Mary, Book 4*.

Magnus was sick to death of Tom and Mary and their insipid adventures. Though he could not read it for himself, he knew it all by heart. He had heard old Miss Mac-

38

farlane going over it a hundred times. Tom and Mary at the sea! Tom and Mary on the farm! Tom and Mary go shopping! Tom and Mary's picnic!

Silly things! They never did anything worthwhile. It suddenly struck Magnus that the book he had left lying on his desk might have some more interesting material in it. *Treasure Island*. It was a good title. Better than Henny-Penny by a long chalk. Better than Tom and Mary and their silly picnics.

'I'll soon be in Book 5,' said Jinty complacently. 'Tom and Mary at the Zoo.'

'Huh,' said Magnus, longing to get up and go, but determined to stick it out. 'Let's see which page you're at.'

Jinty gave a start of surprise. Then all at once she caught on, her woman's intuition coming to the rescue. Of course, that was it! What he wanted was a reading-lesson.

She had more sense than to let him see that she knew.

'You help me, Magnus,' she said, full of guile, turning to the right page and putting another caramel in her mouth. 'One day Tom and Mary packed up their picnic-basket ...'

She went over and over the same words, ones she knew were strange to Magnus, pretending it was she who did not know them. Bit by bit he began to recognize them, hating every moment of the lesson, but feeling the benefit of it, all the same. What a soft lump he was, sitting here with a lassie, doing home-lessons instead of racing about outside, using up his bottled energy! And all because of that pasty-faced schoolmaster.

At last he could stand it no longer and shut the book abruptly. Jinty recognized the signal. The lesson was over.

'You've been a great help to me, Magnus,' she said, as crafty as a serpent. 'I'll see you at the school tomorrow?' It was more a question than a statement.

'Maybe,' he said, and went hurrying away out into the fresh air. But there was no maybe about it.

He was there all right next day, sitting slouched in his seat, feeling like a caged animal. The sun was streaming through the dusty schoolroom window. It was the kind of day when Sula offered everything he liked best – warm sands, the sea-birds lazily resting on the rocks, old Whiskers floating in towards the shore, the intoxicating smell of newly-cut hay – and here he was wasting his time with lessons.

He opened *Treasure Island* and gave a casual glance, recognizing a word here and there. Then he picked up his

pencil, licked the point, and drew a picture of a sea-gull reaching round to peck its tail-feathers. The picture pleased him. It made the book seem less strange. He wrote *Magnus Macduff* on the title page, and was sketching an outline of a seal underneath it, when he was aware of the teacher talking to him.

'Magnus Macduff, are you listening?'

'Uh-huh.'

Andrew Murray stifled a feeling of irritation. He was looking paler this morning. He was going to control this young rebel, no matter what it cost him in nervous energy. He had already won a victory of sorts. The boy had turned up at school.

'What are you doing?' He came towards Magnus, trying to disguise his limp.

'Nothing!' Magnus shut the book with a bang and pushed it aside.

'Come along, Magnus! I want to hear your reading-lesson.'

Magnus flushed. The thought of Henny-Penny was too much for him. For a moment he contemplated bolting out of the schoolroom and escaping into the real world. But to his relief the teacher picked up *Treasure Island* instead. He glanced without comment at the sketches, then pointed to the opening sentence. 'Try it, Magnus. Begin at the beginning.'

The boy gave him one of his direct glances, took a deep breath and began, stumbling, to read. Jinty, squinting over his shoulder at the book, prompted him at intervals in a loud whisper.

'Shut up, you!' he hissed fiercely, whipping round at her. Andrew Murray took no notice of the interruption, and Jinty subsided while Magnus blundered on.

'That's enough! Read some more to yourself. You're doing fine.'

Andrew Murray left him and went to attend to Tair, who was under the desk playing a complicated game with Avizandum. The Ferret, with his catapult back in his pocket, was getting his ammunition ready. A formidable array of inky pellets lay on his desk. But the rest of the class was sitting up and taking notice, looking more alert than in Miss Macfarlane's day. They were not sure yet of the new teacher and his ways.

'Wheesht!' warned Tair, hiding Avizandum in his pocket. 'I'd better not speak to you just now. *He's* got his eye on us.'

Magnus was disappointed to find that the little white dog was not in the classroom. He could hear it yelping

from the schoolhouse next door where the teacher had
left it. Gran was in cleaning, thumping around with
brooms and pails. She had carried a lobster up in her
apron, caught last night by old Cowan – Jinty's grandfather – when he was out with the boats. The pale young
man would have no idea how to cook it, so Gran would
prepare it for him in her competent way, and never say a
word.

Magnus squinted at the blackboard where the teacher
was writing out some simple sums – addition and subtraction. The man was making a fine mess of them!
They were not even in a straight line, and the chalk kept
breaking off and dropping through his fingers on to the
floor. Give *him* a chance and he would have drawn a
lobster crawling all over the blackboard.

The sun beamed in through the window so brightly
that the Ferret abandoned his catapult and took a small
mirror from his pocket instead. It was an old game of his.
Catch the rays of the sun and blind the teacher. But today he was wary. If he turned round, he could blind
Jinty Cowan instead.

'Stop it, you!' She stuck out her tongue at him, and
ducked her head out of reach. She would have flung her
book at his head had she not been in the teacher's line of
vision.

'Pay attention!' rapped Andrew Murray, pointing to
the sums on the blackboard. 'Let's see who can add this
up.'

'Seventeen,' said Tair. He had taken the answer from
Avizandum, but for once *he* was wrong.

'Nonsense!' said the teacher, sharply, 'Magnus Macduff, what do you make it?'

'I haven't thought,' mumbled Magnus.

'Well, think, boy, think!'

Andrew Murray's lips tightened. Then, as a brighter ray shone in through the window, he relaxed and made a sudden decision. Laying down the pointer, he straightened himself up and said, 'Come on! Let's go out!'

A sudden stunned silence. Then, full of self-importance, Jinty put up her hand. 'Please, sir, it's not time.'

'Shut up!' hissed Magnus. Time. What did time matter, if only they could get out into the sunny world? He sat up, and for the first time regarded the teacher with a faint look of respect. *Now* he was talking.

Magnus was the first out, taking a running jump into the air to relieve his spirits. He would have liked to dart off and plunge into the sea beside old Whiskers, if the teacher had not been there, trying to round them up like sheep into his overgrown garden.

'Come along! We can all sit here and continue our lessons.'

The garden was a wilderness of weeds, nettles, a few straggling berry-bushes and clumps of gone-to-seed rhubarb. It was evident that old Miss Macfarlane had given up the struggle and left it all to nature. Andrew Murray stretched himself out under a stunted rowan tree and registered the fact that he must get someone to do some digging for him. In his mind's eye he could see a neat flower-bed, rambler roses trailing over a trellis, perhaps a patch of sweet-peas and a clump of candytuft. He had yet to learn that it was only the hardiest of shrubs – and of human beings – who flourished on the windswept island of Sula.

Not a stir of wind today. The deceitful sun beamed down on them, bringing out the freckles on Jinty's nose, and awakening a white butterfly that went zig-zagging through the air, as if drunk with delight. The children squatted on the ground, taking in gulps of fresh air, elated at the thought of being away from the dingy classroom. In her day, Miss Macfarlane, afraid of draughts, had never opened a window.

Gran emerged from the schoolhouse with the little white dog yelping at her feet. The teacher snapped his fingers. The dog came running unsteadily towards him and sat shivering by her master's side. Without glancing right or left, Gran went stumping away about her business in her big boots.

The children began to giggle and whisper, and to push each other over in the grass. The Ferret found a stinging nettle and pestered the girls' bare legs. Magnus idly pulled up a weed and listened to the open-air sounds – the bleating of a sheep, the call of the sea-birds, the whirr of an aeroplane overhead. It was not easy to concentrate on lessons in such an atmosphere; but who cared about lessons?

Andrew Murray himself would have liked to sit still, letting the sunshine soak into his body, forgetting his responsibilities. He regarded his restless brood, wondering how to capture their attention. Had he been foolish, giving in to his sudden whim to escape from the classroom? No, he would make use of the time. He would tell them a story.

'Long, long ago, before anybody lived on Sula...'

It was a history story, about the beginning of the world, in the days when dinosaurs and other strange prehistoric creatures roamed the land. When he saw the children sitting up, with listening looks on their faces, the teacher began to enjoy himself. He felt a thrill of triumph when he saw that he was holding his audience. Especially when he saw the far-away look fade from Magnus's blue eyes.

The fact that the story was about animals, instead of long-dead kings and queens appealed to the boy. Magnus was illustrating it in his mind's eye with drawings of extinct birds and beasts. What would a pterodactyl be like? Or a dinosaur? Something like old Cowan's goat, with a bigger body and a longer beard? As soon as he had a pencil and a piece of paper he would sketch out what he saw in his imagination. What would Sula have been like with all those big beasts roaming about?

Andrew Murray knew how to tell a tale, how to put colour into his voice, how to use expressive words. Tair – Avizandum forgotten – sat stock-still, taking in every word, whether he understood it or not. The Ferret dropped his stinging-nettle and gave his complete attention to the story. Even the little dog seemed to be listening.

Suddenly the over-bright sun was dimmed by a dark cloud. The wind sprang up and whipped the branches of the rowan-tree. The story stopped abruptly.

'That's it. You can go home now,' said the teacher, dismissing the class. 'I'll tell you the rest in the afternoon.'

'Ooooooh!' said Jinty, voicing the general disappointment. What was a gust of wind? Wait till the teacher had been here long enough to know what a real gale was like.

Reluctantly they got to their feet, lingering in case he changed his mind. But he was pulling his jacket around him, shivering in the wind and hoping to find some comfort – and something to eat – in the schoolhouse.

Before he went in he turned and met the direct gaze of Magnus Macduff. For once the boy's stare was not sullen.

45

'I wonder,' began the teacher, 'do you know anyone who could give me some help in the garden?'

'Uh-huh.'

'Who?'

'I'll see.'

Magnus would not commit himself. The thought crossed his mind that he might do it himself. Maybe. He turned and ran off. He had better not go too far away. He must eat his dinner quickly and get back to school in time to hear the rest of the story about those strange animals.

But when the time came Magnus was not there...

Chapter 5

THE HEATHERY HILL

IT WAS ALL Jinty's fault. The moment she said it, she could have bitten out her tongue. Usually, she was careful to weigh every word where Magnus was concerned.

She had seen the interest in his face as he listened to the teacher telling his story. Remembering the reading-lesson of the night before, she put two and two together.

'He's trying to please the teacher. Isn't it great? He'll come to school regularly. I can give him a reading-lesson every night...'

She darted away after him down to the cottages by the harbour. She was looking forward to her midday dinner. Pehaps her mother would open a tin of tongue, and another of peaches. Mrs Cowan was no great shakes at cooking or baking. Why trouble with so many tinned goods on the shelves? Magnus, likely, would only have buttermilk and oatcakes, with maybe a bit of home-made cheese.

Jinty would have liked to invite him in to share her meal, but that would be going a bit far. All the same, she would risk speaking to him. Think of all the notice he had taken of her yesterday!

'Magnus!'

'Huh.'

He did not bother to turn around. Why should he? It was only Jinty Cowan. Nothing she could say would interest him.

If only she had left it at that.

He was about to disappear into Gran's cottage when she called out, 'Yon was a grand story, wasn't it, Magnus? The teacher left off at the right bit.'

Magnus whipped round. 'What do you mean, the right bit?'

'Well, I mean, to make sure *you'd* come back to hear the rest.' She gave a self-conscious giggle.

That did it. Magnus looked at her – a look that cut her like a knife – then banged away into the house without another word. Jinty bit her lips, and her appetite for tinned peaches faded away.

Magnus was seething with anger. He wasn't going to have lasses like Jinty sniggering at him. Before long they would be calling him teacher's pet. If that was Mr Clever Murray's way of getting round him, he – Magnus – was not going to fall into the trap. The teacher could keep his prehistoric monsters, and find somebody else to dig up his weedy garden.

Gran was out and about on one of her numerous tasks. She had left cheese and oatcakes on the table, and a jug of buttermilk. Magnus drank from the jug, and grabbed a hunk of cheese and a couple of oatcakes. Stuffing them into his mouth as he went, he made off at a great rate, away from the cottages, away from the croft, away from the school, aiming for the Heathery Hill.

'Mag-nus!'

Gran, stamping about with a sack over her head to

keep off the rain, called out to him as he loped along looking neither to right nor to left. But, if he heard her, he paid no heed.

The rain was tailing off to a trickle, and a watery sun was forcing its way through the clouds when he reached the Heathery Hill and started to climb. It was more like an outsize rockery than a hill, with clumps of bracken and heather growing here and there, and patches of wild flowers hiding in odd nooks and crannies. Old Cowan's goat was slithering about on the lower slopes, and a few sure-footed sheep had clambered higher up, searching for something to chew.

Magnus knew the quickest way up – the perpendicular route. There was a zig-zag path for a more leisurely ascent, but the boy wanted to work off his temper. Anger always gave him strength. He hardly noticed that he was climbing. Indeed, he had reached the top by the time the school-bell started to ring.

Ring away! Magnus was still blazing with fury, and not only against Mr Andrew Murray. He was furious at himself for being so easily taken in. The pale-faced teacher must think him a real softie. 'I've got Magnus in the palm of my hand!' No doubt *that* was what he was thinking. Well, he would soon find out his mistake.

Magnus flung himself down on the topmost rock of the craggy hill. It was shaped like a chair. REST AND BE THANKFUL someone had chipped out of the rock in lop-sided letters long, long ago.

Magnus rested, but he was not thankful. Not till the sun had seeped through his body, and the peace of the scene gradually drove the black thoughts from his mind.

He could see the whole world: the island, the sea, the sky, Sula Point, and the seals turning somersaults in the water. It was easy to pick out every landmark: the harbour, the cottages, the church. He could even recognize the people. The woman wobbling along on her bicycle was Mrs Gillies, the District Nurse; and the last of the children trooping into the schoolroom was surely Jinty Cowan, looking around to see if he was coming.

'Not coming! Not coming!' shouted Magnus, inside himself.

He felt in his pocket. Yes, he had a stub of pencil and a crumpled scrap of paper. Feeling happier, he began to

draw an animal he had never seen. It was a strange prehistoric monster, and had a faint look of Mr Andrew Murray about it.

'Where is Magnus Macduff?'

The teacher had fixed his gaze on Jinty, who blushed bright scarlet, knowing full well it was her fault. She half-feared, half-hoped he would send her to look for the truant. But the teacher only tightened his lips and turned back to the problems on the blackboard.

The class was in no mood for sums, not after their high jinks in the garden. The sun was shining again. Why could he not let them out, and continue the story?

Tair stirred in his seat. Avizandum was inciting him to mutiny. 'Go on! Tell him!'

Tair stood up and cleared his throat. 'Please, sir, I don't feel like sums.'

'What?'

Tair stood his ground. 'Please, sir, you said you'd tell us the rest of the story. About the big beasts . . .'

'Sit down!'

Tair sat down with a bump. The Ferret rewarded him for his pains by stuffing an inky piece of blotting-paper down the back of his neck. But the teacher had seen him.

'Come out, you!'

The Ferret, startled, shuffled out from his seat.

'What were you doing just now?'

The Ferret tried to look innocent. 'Please, sir, nothing, sir.'

'Don't tell lies!' The teacher rapped it out so sharply that the Ferret took a step backwards. What a fuss to make over a piece of inky paper! He had done hundreds of worse things in his day. Old Miss Macfarlane would never even have noticed it.

Tair tried to come to his rescue, fishing up the blotting-paper from the back of his neck. 'Please, sir, I don't mind, sir.'

'That's not the point.'

What *was* the point? How could he explain to this unruly brood that, though he wanted to be friendly, he must have discipline? He had already failed with Magnus, after feeling sure he was using the right tactics. He must be firm with the others.

'Empty your pockets!'

The Ferret had only one pocket to empty. The other was held together by a safety-pin, and not strong enough

51

to harbour any of his treasures. Out came his catapult.
Out came a broken knife, a length of tarry twine, and an
unidentified object.

'What's that?'

'Nothing, sir.'

'Don't be ridiculous!' Andrew Murray picked it up
and gazed at it in surprise. 'Where did you find it?'

The Ferret considered. It had been in his pocket so
long, he had almost forgotten where he had found it. He
was about to say, 'Nowhere,' when he remembered.

'The Heathery Hill. That's where I found it.'

Why was the teacher making such a fuss about it? The
man was daft! It was only a piece of stone.

Such a piece of stone as Andrew Murray had never set
eyes on before. A stone sparkling with a hundred subtle
colours. The sky and the sea and the heather were all
there, blended together into a gleaming mass.

'It's beautiful,' he said, turning it over in his hand.
'Beautiful.'

The Ferret scuffled his feet. The man was daft, right
enough. Why was he going on like that about a piece of
stone? There were hundreds like it up on the Hill.

'Are you wanting it?' he asked, not really keen on giving it away. It had been in his pocket so long, it was
almost part of himself.

'No! No, thank you,' said the teacher, coming out of
his reverie. He laid the stone on his desk and sternly told
the Ferret to get back to his place.

All afternoon the stone gleamed and glistened as it
caught the rays of the sun. It was the only sparkling
thing in the classroom. The children seemed more
wooden and stupid as the day wore on. Andrew Murray
felt his temper fraying. He would have liked to punish

the whole lot, and not only by making them empty their pockets.

Avizandum was the only one who escaped.

'I'm away,' he whispered to Tair, and disappeared into his own mysterious world, leaving the boy bereft. He would return when the coast was clear.

The sight of *Treasure Island* lying unheeded on Magnus Macduff's desk gave Andrew Murray a bigger problem than all the sums on the blackboard. Those drawings – and yet, the ignorance and insolence of the boy! He was puzzling how to deal with the young rebel when the door was pushed open without a by-your-leave.

A shabby, elderly man wearing a crumpled grey suit and a dog-collar came in. He looked over his spectacles at the class who shuffled to their feet and greeted him – more or less – in unison.

'Good-afternoon, Mr Morrison!'

They were glad of a diversion, even if it was only the minister. He was a jokey old man, always good for a laugh. They had heard all his quips and jests a hundred times before. Still, he would keep them off their sums.

'Good afternoon, bairns!'

He returned their greeting, then held out his hand to the teacher. 'The Reverend Alexander Morrison. You'll be Mr Murray. Have you skelped them all yet?'

The class began to giggle. 'They could do with a skelping,' said Andrew Murray, with a forced smile. 'It's good of you to call, Mr Morrison.'

'Oh, I like to keep an eye on my flock. Old Miss Mac-farlane used to send for me sometimes when they got out of control. One look from me and they were just as bad as ever.' The class snorted. 'But I expect you'll know how to deal with them.' He eyed the pale young man as if he was not so sure.

'I'll do my best.' Andrew Murray was taking the man's measure. He had an untidy, easy-osy look about him, as if he had given up bothering. Perhaps that was what living on such a small island had done to him. He must watch and not get into the same ways himself. 'About Magnus Macduff,' he started to say, and then stopped. This was not the man to help him with his problems.

'The wee deevil!' The minister chuckled, and the class, listening to every word, chuckled with him. 'I see he's missing again. Oh well, you know what laddies are like. He has to be led, that one, not driven. I'm a bit like that myself. *I* was a wee deevil in my day.'

'You're a great big nothing,' Andrew Murray said – but only to himself. He felt angry at the intruder, standing there getting easy laughs from the class. A great help *he* was going to be.

The minister went over to the blackboard, rubbed out one of the sums and drew a face with a big nose. It was obviously his party-piece. The children giggled as they watched him, and the Ferret felt in his pocket for his catapult. The minister would have made a great target, standing there with his back turned.

'Well, I'm away!' Mr Morrison rubbed his hands together, feeling he had cheered up their dull lives. 'Send for me any time they get out of hand. Union is strength.' He winked at the teacher and then at the children. 'Cheerio, bairns!'

'Cheerio, Mr Morrison!'

When he had gone, Jinty Cowan tried to start a conversation. 'Yon's an awful man,' she giggled, but Andrew Murray did not take her up. He was too busy rubbing out the face on the blackboard.

'Settle down,' he said sternly. 'You're here to work.'

All except Magnus Macduff. But something strange was happening to *him* on the Heathery Hill.

Chapter 6

MR SKINNYMALINK

'Hi, you! Come back. Don't go away. Silly thing.'

Magnus was laughing at the antics of a puffin, surely
the most comical of all sea-birds, who had landed at his

feet and was strutting about in a self-important manner.

The boy began to draw a rapid sketch, longing as he
did so for a paint-box full of colour. How else could he
show the bird's black neck and wings, its white shirt-
front, its beak striped with red and blue, its horny eye-
brows and red legs? It looked like a comedian dressed up
to play a part.

'Wait! I haven't finished yet...' But the puffin ran off sideways and then took to the air in a flurry. 'Okay! Go, then. There are plenty more like you,' said Magnus, putting away his paper and pencil.

He had worked off his bad mood by now. He would run down the other side of the Heathery Hill, past the old cave, and look for driftwood on the sandy beach. There was always something to find on the shore, and maybe he could take a closer look at a puffin, to complete his drawing.

He was slithering down past the cave when he heard a voice echoing from inside.

'Mag-nus!'

'Hullo!'

The boy stopped in his tracks, startled for the moment. Then he remembered. It must be the Hermit. Mr Skinnymalink, they called him on Sula, because he was so long and so lean, and because he had no other name that they knew. Sometimes he stayed in a ramshackle hut at the far end of the island, out of sight and sound; but now and again, for a change, he came and inhabited the cave. He had never been known to speak to a soul, except Magnus.

Magnus understood him. Mr Skinnymalink was, in a way, like old Whiskers. They could sit together for hours, needing no words.

Today the Hermit had something he wanted to say. Magnus peered into the inner darkness of the cave and found him sitting squatting beside a smoky fire. In his hand he held a gleaming stone, like the one in the Ferret's pocket, which he was rubbing and polishing, as if to bring out the colours. It was one of Mr Skinnymalink's hobbies, to collect and polish the stones. He had a small heap beside him, and little hoards hidden all over the island.

Magnus knew better than to speak first. He came in and sat down by the fire, giving the Hermit time to get used to his presence. He took the whistle from his pocket and played a few up-and-down notes. He knew that after a time his companion would take it from him, thump it on his knee, and play a real tune. He had a true ear for music, had Mr Skinnymalink.

The man laid down his stone and reached out for the whistle. Magnus handed it to him and gazed out to the sea and the circling sea-mews as he listened to the music. The Hermit played old sad tunes. Some Magnus had heard before; others the man made up on the spur of the moment. They seemed to have a story to tell, of stormy winds, splashing waves, and the long loneliness of his life on the island.

Presently he laid down the whistle. He was ready to talk.

'What's he like?'

'Him?' Magnus knew fine who he meant. Who else but the new teacher? Mr Skinnymalink was a recluse, but he missed little that went on in Sula. 'He's a queer man, yon,' said Magnus, giving his verdict.

Mr Skinnymalink shot a glance at him, asking for more information.

'He's kind of soft,' said Magnus. "He's got a wee dog . . .'

The Hermit nodded. He had seen the wee dog. He had seen the children, too, seated in a group in the school garden, with Magnus in their midst. That was what had puzzled him, seeing Magnus brought to heel – an obedient scholar. It was not like the boy to be so easily tamed.

Magnus flushed and said fiercely, 'Huh! I can't stand him. Nor the school.' He looked enviously at the Hermit. 'I wish I was like you.' Freedom was the thing!

Mr Skinnymalink laughed. It was seldom he did. The sound of it startled him. Fancy anyone wanting to be like him. What must he look like? He had not seen himself for years.

He felt his face. His beard was rough and matted. His hair straggled down to his shoulders. As for his clothes, a scare-crow would have been better dressed. His trousers were ragged and torn. His jacket was a cast-off of Gran's, and when Gran cast off a garment it had done more than its spell of duty. Not that he cared for clothes. Had he not come here to escape from tailored suits and traffic and artificial people? He had almost forgotten what the outside world was like.

Magnus did not notice the rags or the unkempt hair. The Hermit was part of the landscape, as familiar as a dry-stone dyke – and as uncommunicative. They had all long ago given up wondering who he was or why he wanted to be by himself. He had stepped off the steamer one day with a pack on his back, and that was that. No questions asked or answered.

Gran, in her strange way, saw to it that he did not starve. Sometimes she took parcels of food – scones, cheese, oatcakes and butter – to his hut and left them there, no words spoken. Not that he looked for help. Mr Skinnymalink knew how to fend for himself, fishing, fowling, and finding wild berries in season. He still had a hoard of money, too, which he doled out piecemeal to Magnus when he needed groceries from the Cowans' shop. He grew some vegetables beside his hut, and asked for nothing better than to be left alone.

If Gran brought him milk or meat, he saw to it that she was repaid, He would gather driftwood from the shore and pile it up at her door; or leave some fish which he had caught. Or he would spend hours digging up her peat. Gran took no notice of him, but accepted his offerings without a word. He was there on the island, and yet not there, moving about as if he was an invisible man.

Yet he noticed everything.

'Where does he come from?' he asked suddenly, still on the subject of the young schoolmaster.

'Glasgow, I think,' said Magnus. He could come from Timbuctoo, for all the boy cared. 'I wish he would go back,' he burst out.

They sat in silence for awhile. Then Magnus asked, 'Have you ever heard of a terry-something? A terrydactil?'

'A what?'

'It's a beast. A prehistoric monster.'

'A pterodactyl. Oh yes, I've heard of it.'

'Fancy!' Magnus gazed at the Hermit with new respect. 'What was it like?'

Mr Skinnymalink cleared his throat. His voice was hoarse through lack of use; but once he started to speak, the flow went on. He covered the same ground as the teacher had done earlier in the day. Then he went on to tell of other strange birds and beasts, long since extinct. Magnus saw them all in his imagination. A dodo! Now, that must have been a queer beast. Funnier even than a puffin.

As for Andrew Murray, he could keep his stories. Magnus knew as much now as he did, maybe more. 'I wish you were the teacher,' he told the Hermit.

Mr Skinnymalink threw back his head and laughed for

 the second time that day. The laugh ended in a fit of coughing, and that was that. The man withdrew into his shell. The shut-down look came over his face, and Magnus did not need to be told that the session was ended. It would be days, or weeks maybe, before the Hermit uttered another word.

'Any messages?' Magnus asked, before he took his leave.

The Hermit shook his head. He did not look up. He was absorbed once more in polishing the sparkling stone.

There was no problem about going to school or staying away from it next day. It was Saturday, a holiday for some, but not for Magnus. Gran had given her orders.

'Mag-nus! Fetch the black-faced sheep! We'll take them across to Little Sula.'

Gran got the boat ready while Magnus ran to round-up the three black-faced sheep. Silly things! they had wandered up to the lower slopes of the Heathery Hill, trying to find a fresh bite between the clumps of bracken and heather.

'Come on! You'll get plenty to eat on Little Sula.'

It was only a dot in the water, a dot which sometimes disappeared when the big seas swept over it in stormy weather. But there was good grazing on it in the summer. The islanders made full use of the fresh grass, rowing their animals across for a change of diet, and watching the weather carefully in case the wind blew up.

Sometimes a hasty rescue had to be organized. There

was the time when old Cowan's goat was marooned and set up such a bleating that they had to launch the lifeboat to bring him back. He hated getting his feet wet, did Bilko!

Magnus drove the sheep down to the harbour. Jinty was there with her skipping-rope, counting out in a sing-song voice the old Pictish numbers: 'Een-teen-tethera-methera . . .'

She broke off when she saw Magnus and called, 'Yoo-hoo!' in a hopeful voice; but Magnus took no notice of her.

Tair was there, too, making aeroplane noises as he zoomed along the harbour-wall, ready for take-off. Luckily, he stopped in time, or maybe it was Avizandum who

warned him, otherwise he would have been over into the sea, and not for the first time.

Getting the sheep into the boat was a tricky operation. The Ferret lent a hand, wading up to his knees as he pushed the boat off from the shore. He would have given Magnus a parting box in the ears – partly in fun and partly in earnest – if Gran had not been there with her eye on him. She could floor him with a look.

The old woman rowed with a steady stroke – in-out, in-out – her sinewy arms never flagging. Magnus held on to the sheep, keeping them steady and saving them from tumbling overboard. There was no conversation. Gran did not waste time speaking unless there was something special to say.

A flurry of oyster-catchers and gulls came flying out from Little Sula to greet them, circling and screaming overhead, annoyed at having their desert-island disturbed. They were like the Hermit, and yet unlike. They wanted to be free – free to herd together with their own kind.

Today they had cause for complaint. Another intruder had gate-crashed their domain.

'Look, Gran! There's a boat there already!'

'So I see! The Cowans' boat!'

Gran's sharp eyes noted everything. There were no Cowans in the boat. Only one man struggling to beach it on the small shingly shore, and making a fine mess of it, too!

'Huh, it's *him*,' said Magnus in a disgusted voice. The day was ruined.

The young schoolmaster had obviously underestimated the effort it would take to row himself across to the little island. He had meant to explore Sula itself on this fine Saturday morning, but his leg was hurting. It would not be easy for him to walk far. Easier, he thought, to take his camera and row across to Little Sula to photograph the sea-birds. The small island had been luring him since ever he set eyes on it.

He had done some rowing in his day. His arms were strong enough. Even so, he was out of practice – and out of breath – by the time he had made the short crossing.

'Hold on,' Gran called out in her deep voice. 'The boy'll help you.'

It was the last thing Magnus wanted to do. Let him

help himself. He had enough on his own hands, getting the sheep on to dry land. They slipped and slithered while Magnus half-pushed, half-carried them off the boat. Once ashore, they wasted no time before browsing amongst the clumps of sea-pinks to find their first bite of fresh grass.

The little white dog had come with her master. She was sitting shivering and shaking in the boat, crying softly to herself like a baby. Magnus had no desire to help the man, but he could not resist the dog.

'Hold on! I'm coming!'

The young teacher looked up as the boy came forward. 'I'm very grateful...' he began; but Magnus pushed him aside.

'I'll manage myself,' he said gruffly.

It was easier tugging the boat in without his ineffectual help.

'Come on, you,' Magnus said to the dog, and lifted her out on to dry land. 'There. You're safe.'

She looked up at him, wagging her tail, reassured by his tone. Frisking at his feet, she was ready to play any game he fancied. Magnus bent down to pat her. She was a silly wee thing, but there was something appealing about her. He would have played with her, if she had not belonged to *him*.

Andrew Murray was sitting by the shore, trying to recover his lost energy. He was angry at himself for having been caught once more at a disadvantage in front of Magnus Macduff. The boy must think him a weakling, right enough.

Gran, her mission completed, was getting ready to go. 'Are you all right?' she called to the teacher.

'Yes, fine!' He tried to make his voice sound bright.

'I'll stay on for a bit and take some photographs.'

'Right! The boy can stay with you and row you back.'

'Oh, Gran!' Magnus cried out in dismay. But she had pushed her boat off and was already dipping the oars into the water. She had given her orders, and that was that.

The angry gulls and gannets screamed after her; but there was no one on the island angrier than Magnus Macduff left alone with the schoolmaster.

Chapter 7

THE PAINTED YACHT

'MAGNUS!'

'What?'

Magnus looked as dour as a drystone dyke. If the teacher was going to lecture him, he would jump into the sea and swim for home. So he would! He could do it; rock to rock. Anyway, he would as soon risk drowning as stay on Little Sula at the mercy of that man's tongue.

But Andrew Murray was not in a lecturing mood. He was too absorbed with his camera. 'Do you know anything about taking photographs?' he asked the boy, determined to let bygones be bygones.

'No!'

End of conversation, as far as Magnus was concerned. What was a photograph compared to a drawing? Let the man get on with it. *He* was not going to show any interest.

'Oh well,' said the teacher mildly, 'perhaps you'll keep an eye on Trix.'

The little dog, in a sudden fit of boldness, had run off to join the sheep. One of them – the biggest and blackest – stopped cropping the grass to take a look at her.

Who was this queer creature with the curly coat and spindly legs? Not a lamb, surely. Certainly not a collie dog. Friend or foe? It was difficult to tell.

Blackie let out a loud questioning bleat. That was enough for Trixie. She gave a frightened yelp and turned tail so suddenly that she tumbled head-over-heels, rolling down the grassy slope into Magnus's arms.

The boy grinned as he caught her. 'Silly wee thing. They're only sheep.'

He held the small shivering creature in his arms till she calmed down. 'There! You're fine. Come on. We'll take a walk.'

The walk had to be short. A few hundred yards one way. A few hundred yards the other way. Up a little hillock – and that was it. The dog looked back to see if her master was following, but he was still busy with his camera. All right. She would go off without him, keeping close to the boy's heels and well out of reach of the black-faced monster.

'Come on, wee dog. Step into the Fairy Ring.'

It was at the top of the little hillock, a complete circle on the grass. Magnus lifted the little animal and placed her in position.

'There! Wish a wish!'

The dog stood in the circle, looking up at him, wondering what it was all about. Magnus stepped in beside her to wish a wish for himself.

'I wish . . .'

What could he wish for? He already had everything he wanted. Money? What could he buy with it, except maybe a box of paints? Health? He was lucky enough to have that already. Peace? Yes, that was what he needed most. Even on such an isolated island as Sula, he could never get enough.

He looked back at the schoolmaster clicking away with his camera, and frowned. The disturber of his peace.

'I wish *he* would go and...'

A strange feeling, almost like an electric shock, shot through his body. The little dog, too, began to quake and quiver. Magnus, alarmed, put the wish hastily out of his mind and stepped from the ring.

It was all nonsense, of course. He did not believe the old tales the islanders told of the Fairy Ring and how wishes came true. Especially evil wishes. The Ferret's grandfather, so they said, had ill-wished his own brother. True enough, the man's cow had died, his crops had failed, and he himself fell sick of a strange disease from which he never recovered.

There were tales, too, of fishermen who had been lost in sudden storms; of children born deformed; of old women going blind – and all because of an ill-wish in the Fairy Ring.

Remembering this and other old tales, Magnus hastily stepped back into the circle, and, to be on the safe side, muttered, 'I wish him no harm...'

As if he had heard, Andrew Murray called out to him: 'Magnus!'

'What?'

'Would you like to come and have your photograph taken?'

'No!'

It was the kind of No Jinty Cowan would have recognized as final. Andrew Murray recognized it, too, and felt his anger rising; but he let it pass. He was not going to spoil this sunny day by quarrelling with a silly young schoolboy. Let him stay in his prickly shell.

He turned his attention to the sea-birds, instead, trying to find out the best way to capture them in his camera as they landed and took off. Was that a razorbill? Magnus would know, but what was the use of asking *him*?

As the sun rose higher he began to feel a glow of health, as if new life was flowing back into his veins. A great desire came over him to leap and run, as Magnus was doing. If only he could!

He dragged himself up to the rop of the hillock. 'Goodness! A Fairy Ring!' He was talking to himself, for the boy, seeing him coming, had wandered back to the seashore. 'I wonder if it would work?'

He stood in the centre, closed his eyes tightly, and wished. No need to wonder what *he* desired most. 'Let me be strong again and healthy. *Please!*'

The wish was so intense that he felt sure a miracle must happen. Yet when he opened his eyes he was the same as before. No transformation; but the faint feeling of well-being was still there, as if the sun and air had already begun its slow healing. 'Perhaps through time,' he thought, and went limping back to join the boy at the water's edge.

On the way down his eye was attracted by a glittering object on the ground – a small stone glinting in the sunshine with all the colours of the rainbow.

'Look! See what I've found!' He let out a boyish shout of excitement as he stooped to pick it up.

'Huh!'

Magnus took one look at the stone and turned away. The Hermit had hundreds of them. They were all over the place. What a fuss to make about nothing!

The teacher was looking at the stone as if he had just found a priceless treasure. He rubbed it carefully on his jacket sleeve and then put it away in his pocket. At least he was upsides with the Ferret now.

Magnus was anxious to get away. If he had been alone, he would have stayed long enough on the little island. Maybe old Whiskers would have joined him, and then they would have lain in peace together soaking in the sunshine. But he felt uneasy being at such close quarters with the teacher.

'It's time we were away,' he muttered, lifting the little dog into the boat. If the man was coming, he had better hurry up. Otherwise, he would be left behind.

Andrew Murray hurried as well as he could, wondering if he should offer to lend a hand with the boat. Wondering, too, if he might make a last attempt to penetrate the boy's defences. No! One look at Magnus's face warned him that it would be better not to try.

They cast off in silence. Magnus took both oars, not giving his passenger a chance to help. In-out; he rowed with a steady stroke, his strong arms so co-ordinated that the boat made quick progress. Soon they were rounding the point towards home.

As Andrew Murray gazed at the Heathery Hill coming closer, he saw a gaunt figure disappear into a cave on the cliff-side.

'Who's that,' he asked, startled.

'Nobody.'

Magnus had seen Mr Skinnymalink but had no intention of giving him away.

The teacher felt his anger rising. He had controlled it long enough. He – a grown man – was not going to be treated like this by such an insolent young puppy. It was time to assert himself.

'Don't be ridiculous, boy!' he burst out in his most schoolmasterly voice. 'Nobody, indeed! It was a man. I saw him going into the cave...'

He met Magnus's blank gaze and tried hard to keep a grip on himself. 'Look here, Magnus,' he said, changing his tone, 'what's wrong with you? Why can't you learn to be a little more civil? I'm not your enemy, you know. I'd much rather be your friend. But surely you must realize that there are certain rules in life that must be obeyed. Going to school, for example. And telling the truth. As for the man in the cave, what's the point of making a mystery? If you won't tell me about him, somebody else will...'

He might have been speaking to the wind. Magnus was not listening. The boat wobbled for a moment as the boy gazed out to sea. His keen eye had caught sight of a ship. Not the *Hebridean*, surely. She was not due for another few days. This looked like a yacht. Whose could it be, the boy wondered – hearing, and yet not hearing the teacher's admonishing words?

'So I expect you to be in your place on Monday. No more playing truant,' he ended up, knowing full well that nothing he had said had reached its mark.

He felt suddenly deflated. His brief burst of health seemed to have left him. When he reached the shore he could scarcely heave himself out of the boat. As he stumbled on to the shingly sand he was aware of young Jinty Cowan buzzing about like an excited bumble-bee. She had a self-important look on her face and was clutching something in her hand.

'It's a tellygram, Mr Murray!'

'A what?'

'A tellygram!' She waved it at him like a flag. 'It came through the tellyphone. For you.'

Jinty knew what was inside it and was bursting to tell someone. Preferably Magnus. What was the use of knowing something if she could not show her superiority?

'Magnus!' she hissed at him as he pulled the boat on to the shingle. 'D'you want to know what the tellygram says?'

It was a silly thing to ask. His only answer would be No. In any case, he was more interested in the yacht. There was no doubt about it, it was making for Sula. With its cream-coloured paint and bright red sails, it looked more like a toy than a real ship. Very different from the sturdy *Hebridean*.

Jinty had seen it, too. 'That's what the tellygram's about. The yacht!'

'What?'

At lasy she had captured his interest. She gabbled out the message. 'Coming in the yacht to Sula. Hope to do some filming. See you soon, Jeremy.'

She waited to see the effect. It took some time to sink in. Magnus felt a surge of excitement, and then a feeling of dismay. There would be no peace on the island now with a crowd of inquisitive strangers poking their cameras into every corner. Another black mark to the teacher! It was all his fault.

Andrew Murray was as little pleased at the prospect as Magnus. He re-read the telegram hoping he might have made a mistake. No. There it was in Mrs Cowan's scratchy writing. *See you soon, Jeremy.*

He had never been over-fond of his cousin. They had little in common except their shared name. Their fathers had been brothers; but they, too, were of different temperaments. Sir David – Andrew's father – was a hardheaded business-man who had literally worked himself to death. Uncle Andrew, who had been his partner in the engineering firm, had no liking for sitting at a desk.

He would disappear for long stretches of time, 'on business overseas'. The trips lasted longer and longer. Finally, after his wife's death, they lasted so long that he disappeared altogether, leaving his son Jeremy in control of the business.

Jeremy and business did not go together.

'Poor Jeremy, it's not his fault. It's his artistic temperament.' Lady Rose Murray had a soft spot for her nephew. 'You can't blame him. He has so many talents. He doesn't know which to concentrate on.'

That was the trouble. Jeremy had a bent for everything except engineering. Music. Drama. Art. He dabbled in them all, while the business chugged along as best it could, with the help of Mr Menzies, the manager.

'Look! They're dropping the anchor.'

It was Avizandum who told Tair, though he could see it plainly enough for himself.

They were all down at the harbour – the McLeods, the Cowans, the McCallums, the District Nurse, the minister, Gran, even Bilko the goat, watching the painted yacht coming closer.

By now they all knew the contents of the telegram. It was difficult to keep a secret on Sula, especially with such a chatterbox as Jinty Cowan to spread the news.

'It's someone Mr Murray knows! His name's Jeremy! He's coming to make a fillum! Fancy, we'll all be in it!'

Jinty was already dressed for her role as film-star. She

had rushed home to put on her best frock, the one her mother had made from a pattern in a fashion magazine. It was blue velvet, and would have looked nice and neat enough if Mrs Cowan had not added so many touches here and there to 'liven it up'. A lace collar. Little pink bows scattered over the skirt. A row of silvery buttons down the front. Another lace flounce at the hem.

Jinty herself had added the final touch by tying a pink ribbon from a chocolate-box round her hair. Now she was perfect! If only she had a pair of high-heeled shoes.

Who could resist her? She prinked and preened, waiting for compliments. But flattery was a rare commodity on Sula. The Ferret stuck out his tongue at her. The District Nurse took one look and turned her head away. The Reverend Alexander Morrison was the only one to make any comment. 'My, what a sight!' he said in his jokey way; but whether it was a compliment or not, Jinty was not sure.

Undaunted, she stood posing on the shore. The film-unit would be sure to see her and pick her out from the rest. 'Look! There she is. The very one we've been looking for. A ready-made heroine.'

She hoped Magnus had noticed her and was admiring her finery. Not he. The boy was apart from the rest as usual, sitting on his favourite rock, jutting out to sea. Not a sight of Whiskers – not that Magnus expected to see him. The old seal had more sense than to surface in the midst of so much commotion.

Magnus thought of the Fairy Ring and his wish for peace. There would be less than ever now on the island. He looked up at the Heathery Hill wondering if Mr Skinnymalink was watching from the cave. He would be as disturbed as Magnus at the thought of strangers invading his quiet refuge.

A small boat had set off from the yacht and was coming in to the shore. Two figures inside it. Magnus could not make them out. Were they a man and a girl? Both were dressed alike in jeans and duffel coats.

A cry of dismay from Jinty. The teacher's dog, prancing about at the water's edge, had jumped up on her with wet paws.

'Oh!' she wailed. 'Look what a dirty mess you've made of my good frock.'

She stepped hastily back to avoid further contact with the dog. The next moment she had lost her balance and tumbled on to the wet sand. The incoming boat sent a wave splashing towards her; and there she sat in her wet finery for all to see, her face begrimed with tears.

The Ferret cackled with unkind laughter. 'Ahoy there, Andrew!' came a shout from the boat; and Jinty looked up through her tears to see a tall young man waving to the teacher. Beside him sat a young woman, blonde and beautiful, looking like a real film-star. The sight of her made Jinty's tears flow faster. It was the last straw!

Chapter 8

THE HANGMAN'S WHIP

'Yes, I will. No, I won't. Maybe I will. Maybe I won't. Yes. No. Maybe...'

Magnus was playing a game with himself as he sat at the kitchen table supping his breakfast porridge. Should he or shouldn't he go to school on this fine Monday morning? Yes. No. Maybe.

No matter what the answer was it did not satisfy him. It was like tossing a coin and hoping it came down edgeways.

There was a small bowl of creamy milk by the side of his porridge-plate into which he dipped his spoon, time and about. Yes. No. Maybe. No one on Sula would have dreamed of spoiling their porridge by pouring milk straight on to it. There was a certain ritual in eating it as well as in making it.

Gran's porridge was never lumpy. No knot could survive the vigorous stirring she gave it each morning with the wooden spirtle, so hard-worked that it was almost worn away. The porridge had the right amount of salt in it – never too much nor too little – which brought out its nutty flavour, though Gran did it by guess-work.

77

'A good lining to your stomach,' she declared.

The Hermit's methods were much simpler. He made a concoction called *brose* simply by pouring boiling water on the oatmeal, stirring some salt into it, and – hey presto! – his meal was ready.

Magnus had heard how hill sheperds, living along in remote cottages, made a week's supply of porridge and poured it into a drawer. When it cooled they cut out solid lumps to take with them and eat as they were herding the sheep.

Magnus preferred Gran's. She had been up and about for hours. So had he, for that matter. He had fed the hens, rounded up the sheep, and brought in the day's supply of peat. He had also gathered the half-dozen brown eggs that were now lying on the kitchen table.

There was evidence on the table, too, that Gran had done a batch of baking before going out to milk the cow. Floury scones were set up on their sides to cool. A large barley-bannock sat beside them, and a wire tray full of golden pancakes. *Dropscones*, Gran called them.

The boy was surprised to see such a tempting array. It was not often Gran baked anything as fancy as dropscones. Maybe they were for the gentry on the painted yacht. Magnus contemplated eating one, but if he knew Gran she would have them counted. Yes! No! Maybe!

He had finished his porridge, but still not made up his mind, when the door was pushed open and Jinty Cowan came in, followed by a speckled hen. There were no such ceremonies as knocking at doors on Sula, or about locking them. Indeed, they were often enough left wide open. Privacy was not easily achieved.

'Hullo, Specky! Help yourself.'

Magnus ignored Jinty and spoke to the hen who was pecking hopefully on the floor. She was a lone bird, belonging to nobody in particular. Specky fed where she could, and roamed foot-loose all over the island, laying her eggs were she fancied. Sometimes she took a notion for human company and wandered in at an open door. Now and then she appeared in the schoolroom. Her picture was in Magnus's reading-book, along with Henny-Penny and her silly shopping-basket.

Jinty stood in the doorway in her old skirt and faded jersey, no longer the glamorous film-star. Today her hair was unbrushed; she had a flushed look on her face and was coughing violently.

'Hear that, Magnus?' Cough! Cough! Cough! 'I've got a chill! I'm not to go to the school. The District Nurse is coming to see me. Will you tell the teacher?'

'What?' Magnus looked up, startled at the prospect of telling the teacher anything. 'I might not be going.'

'Oh well.' Jinty was feeling too ill to care. She took another fit of coughing. 'If you see the Ferret or any of the others, will you tell them? I'm supposed to be in my bed.'

'Okay,' said Magnus. He felt sorry for her but he was not going to say it. 'I'll see.'

Jinty sighed and said hopefully, 'Maybe you'll look in and see me later on?'

'Maybe.'

She hovered for a moment, waiting for a crumb of comfort. None was forthcoming, so she gave another cough and trailed herself away.

Specky had settled down on the rag rug by the fire, looking as if she might be going to lay an egg. Maybe Gran would give it to Magnus to take to Mr Skinny-

malink with some of her newly-baked scones. Yes! No!
Maybe!

The school bell began to ring. He must make up his
mind; now or never. Perhaps he had better go and be
done with it. He could just sit at his desk and not bother
to work. If he put in an appearance now, he could slip
away for the afternoon.

He left Specky in possession and went, half-running,
up to the school. He could see the painted yacht rocking
gently on the water, but no sign of life on board. Magnus
wondered what had happened to the man Jeremy and
yon girl with the blonde hair. They would be coming
ashore again, likely, with their cameras and fancy talk.
'Away you go,' he shouted inside himself. 'Leave us in
peace.'

The bell had stopped ringing by the time he slipped in
to his seat. Andrew Murray was calling out the register.

'Here, sir!'

'Present!'

'Yes!'

The pupils replied in their different ways. In old Miss
Macfarlane's day they had tried all sorts of tricks. Sometimes they answered in squeaky voices, or in deep
growls, or even hooted like owls. The Ferret sometimes
barked or attempted a yodel. It was always good for a
giggle. But things were different now.

'Magnus Macduff!'

'Present,' mumbled Magnus, slouching in his seat and
trying to look as un-present as possible. The teacher took
no notice of him, but went on to the next name.

'Janet Cowan!'

Silence.

Andrew Murray looked up and saw that her seat was

empty. 'Where's Jinty?' he asked in a general way.

'Absent,' said Magnus in a gruff voice.

'So I see,' The teacher tried to speak mildly. 'Can anyone tell me what's worng with her?'

A pause; then Magnus muttered, 'She's got a chill.'

'Oh, has she, poor girl? Thanks for letting me know, Magnus. If you see her, tell her I hope she'll soon be better. Now, get on with your reading.'

Magnus went through the motions of obeying him. Thank goodness, the man hadn't told him to read aloud. Without Jinty to prompt him, he would have made a poor show. He pushed his old book aside and opened *Treasure Island* but did not bother to read the words. Instead, he tried to turn the capital letters into pictures. C was easily converted into a crab. In next to no time D became the speckled hen and S a rabbit sitting up on its hindlegs.

It was better fun than worrying about words. What were words compared with pictures? How easy it must have been to read, in the old days when people did not bother with books. They just drew pictures on the walls of their caves. So the Hermit had told him.

Magnus was so absorbed that he did not notice the teacher had left his desk and was bending over him.

'How are you getting on, Magnus?'

'Fine,' said Magnus, shutting the book.

Andrew Murray bit back a sharp word and passed on to the next desk. Ignore the silly boy. He could capture his attention later on by continuing the story he had begun in the schoolhouse garden.

'What are *you* doing?' he asked Tair who was staring out of the window at nothing in particclar.

'Watch it!' warned Avizandum, from his pocket. 'Say you're thinking.'

'Please, sir, I'm thinking.'

Andrew Murray gave him an amused look. 'What about?'

What about! Avizandum made several suggestions which Tair discarded. The moon. Rice-pudding. Jack, the Giant-Killer.

'I'm just thinking.'

'Oh well, there's nothing wrong with that,' said the teacher, smiling at him. 'Let's all do our thinking together. You remember the story I was telling you ...'

'Oh yes, sir; please, sir!' The class showed its approval. With one abstainer. Magnus did not even look up.

'The big beasts,' said the Ferret, letting the teacher know that *he* remembered. He was keeping his hands in his pockets in case his few treasures were confiscated. He had a new one today, a small field-mouse which he had found on his way to school. He had saved its life. At least, he had not given way to his first impulse to kill it. For the moment, it was his proudest possession.

'Take your hands out of your pockets and sit up straight,' the teacher told him severely.

The Ferret took his hands out for a second, then put them back again. He liked feeling the small creature

83

quivering at his mercy. He would be kind to it. Maybe he would set it free once he was outside. Or maybe he would put it down the neck of one of the girls to make her squeal.

The teacher was re-capping on the story-lesson he had given them in the garden. "You remember what I told you ...'

'Yes, yes! Get on with it!' thought Magnus impatiently. He was pretending not to listen. *He* was one step ahead of the teacher and the rest of the class. 'Come on! Tell us the next bit – about the stegosaurus.'

He had no idea how to spell it, but he had a vague picture of what it looked like, from the Hermit's description. He doodled it down on a piece of paper torn from his exer-cise-book – an enormous lizard with great spikes on its back. The teacher, talking on, caught sight of him from the corner of his eye. That boy again!

'Magnus Macduff! What are you doing?'

Magnus hastily covered the drawing with his hand and gave the usual answer: 'Nothing.'

'Stupid boy!' Andrew Murray could stand it no longer. 'Come out at once and bring that piece of paper with you.'

Magnus hesitated. For a moment he thought of tearing up the drawing and making a dash for the door. There was no peace nowadays with that man always on top of him.

The teacher lifted up the lid of the old desk and fumbled about inside. The children gave a gasp when they saw what he brought to light. The hangman's whip!

The Ferret turned white at the sight of it, and Avizandum did a quick disappearing act. If *that* thing was coming out, the school was no place for him.

It was made of leather with thick thongs that could sting and smart when applied to the bare flesh. Some called it the strap, or the tawse, but the children knew – and feared it – by its old name.

Once in a while, driven to desperation, old Miss Macfarlane had threatened them with the hangman's whip, but they knew fine she would never use it. Not her, with her kind heart. But the new teacher was grasping it in a way that meant business.

'I'm waiting!' He spoke in a commanding voice and hit the desk with the hangman's whip. *Thud-thud-thud!* 'Come, Magnus!'

Magnus crumpled the paper in his hand and shuffled out from his desk. The Ferret gave him a shove as he passed, which sent him sideways. Magnus glared at him and laid the creased paper down on the teacher's desk.

Without comment Andrew Murray took it up and straightened it out; and at once his irritation gave way to surprise. He had expected a drawing, of course, but not one as realistic, and at the same time as imaginative as this. The clumsy creature seemed almost to be crawling across the crumpled paper. He wondered if Magnus knew what it was he had drawn.

'Is it the dinosaur I was telling you about?'

Magnus gave his head a slight shake.

'What is it, then?'

'A beast.'

'I can see it's a beast. What kind of beast?'

'Prehistoric,' mumbled Magnus.

'D'you know its name?'

85

'Uh-huh.'

Andrew Murray shot him an angry glance. 'I've had about enough of you, Magnus Macduff! If you know the name, tell me at once! Come on; out with it!'

Magnus shuffled his feet. He was not sure of the name by now, but he had better say something. 'Stego ... stego ...'

'Stegosaurus?'

'Uh-huh.'

Andrew Murray stared at the drawing and then at the boy. 'How did you know?' Had *he* told him? No! he distinctly remembered talking about pterodactyls and dinosaurs, and thinking, 'I'll leave the stegosaurus till next time.' Indeed, he had just been on the point of describing it to the class. Magnus could not have read about it, not with his lack of ability. How then had he found out? 'Who told you about it?'

A stubborn look came over the boy's face. Let the man mind his own business! 'Nobody,' he muttered.

The ding-dong duel continued, with the class listening attentively to every word, wondering who was going to win. Old Miss Macfarlane would have given in long ago; but Andrew Murray – weakling though he was in his body – seemed made of sterner stuff. He had reached the cross-roads with Magnus. Now or never he must show his supremacy.

He tightened his lips and took up the hangman's whip. 'Hold out your hand.'

Magnus blinked his eyes, not in fear, but in surprise. Imagine the man going to such a length? As if he could hurt *him* with his tawse. Magnus could twist it out of his grasp with one flick of his wrist, if he wanted.

The Ferret let out a snort. The girls put their hands to

their mouths to stifle their cries of suspense. If Jinty had been present, there was no knowing to what lengths she might have gone to save the situation.

'Do you hear me, Magnus? Hold out your hand!'

The light of battle was in Andrew Murray's eyes. Yet, as Magnus thrust out his hand, he knew this was no way to win a fight. The boy would only despise him the more.

He raised the hangman's whip – but the blow was never struck. Two diversions happened at the same time. A loud squeal came from one of the girls as the Ferret's mouse escaped from his pocket and went scuttling across the floor. It paused as it reached the blackboard, looking round for a way of escape, and Magnus stooped to pick it up in his unpunished hand. Quickly he transferred it to his pocket. It would be safer there than in the Ferret's.

At the same moment the door opened and two figures appeared – the two from the painted yacht. The blonde girl made a colourful picture, standing in the drab room with the teacher's dog in her arms. She was wearing scarlet jeans today, with a matching kerchief round her head. She looked like some bright bird who had flown in from a far-away exotic land.

The man, too, was decked out in gay plumage. He wore a light blue jersey, sand-coloured trousers, and a yellow scarf round his neck. Small wonder that the pupils sat up and took notice. What a morning they were having!

'Sorry to disturb you,' said the girl, flashing a smile at Andrew Murray. 'I found your little dog outside the door. Are we in the way?'

The teacher had struggled to his feet, the hangman's whip still in his hand. There was a flush on his face as he met the girl's glance. 'In the way? No, not at all! It's a pleasure . . .'

'We've been having a look round the place,' broke in her companion, the man called Jeremy. 'Marvellous! Just the right atmosphere. So wild and remote. It's got everything we need – except a bit of human interest.' He took a look round the classroom at the intent faces watching him. 'What we're looking for is a boy to be the focal point of the film.'

The blonde girl nudged him. She had been watching Magnus standing slim and straight by the teacher's desk. There was a wild and untamed look about him, like Sula itself.

The man turned and looked him over with an appraising glance. Then he cried out, 'That's the one! *He*'ll do!'

Chapter 9

A MIDNIGHT ADVENTURE

'GO BACK TO your seat, Magnus!'

Andrew Murray did not seem to have heard what Jeremy was saying. He was still feeling flustered. The presence of the blonde girl had thrown him off-balance.

He had met her for the first time last night, but already she had made a deep impression on him. What a picture she made standing there with the dog in her arms! How could anyone help admiring her beauty, her cheerfulness, and her direct manner? Lucky Jeremy!

Diana Maxwell was no fluttering film-star. Indeed, she had nothing at all to do with the film world.

'I'm only a passenger,' she had told Andrew. 'I just came along for the ride – never could resist boats or islands – but Jeremy's making me work my passage. So now I'm assistant-producer or camera-man, or something.' She flashed a smile at him. 'History's really my subject, as ancient as possible. I'm actually writing a book. Perhaps I'll find some material on Sula.'

What a girl, though Andrew Murray, more conscious than ever of his own defects. Cousin Jeremy certainly had all the luck.

He was suddenly aware that he was still holding the hangman's whip in his hand, and that Magnus, mouse in pocket, was on his way back to his seat. He dropped the strap on to the desk, while Jeremy called out: 'Wait, boy! I want to speak to you. What's your name?'

Magnus half-turned to look at him, and then gave a reluctant reply: 'Magnus Macduff.'

'Well, Magnus, how would you like to be in a film?'

The rest of the class let out an 'Oooooooh!' of envy. Fancy Magnus being on the screen! The lucky thing!

But all that Magnus said was, 'No, thank you,' as he turned away and sat down at his desk.

'What do you mean – no, thank you,' said the man, in a cross voice. He was not used to such treatment. The very opposite. 'There are hundreds of boys who would jump at the chance . . .'

'Me, sir,' said the Ferret, putting up his hand.

'Me, sir,' said the others, following suit.

Magnus kept his hand in his pocket, caressing the quivering mouse. He was longing to take it out, examine it closely, draw a picture of it and then set it free. As for the man and his film, let him get on with it.

'D'you mean to say you don't *want* to be in a film?' The man could not believe it!

'Uh-huh,' said Magnus – and that was as much as he intended to say.

'You'll get no change out of *him*,' said Andrew Murray wearily. 'Let's go into the schoolhouse and have a quiet talk. It's time to break for lunch.' It had been a very upside-down morning. They would have to make up for it in the afternoon. 'All right, children. You can go home now. Be back sharp this afternoon.'

He gave Magnus a keen look which was lost on the

90

boy. He was too busy pushing his way past the others, out into the fresh, free air. Goodbye, school!

The girl had caught sight of the crumpled drawing on the desk. 'I say, who drew this? The boy Magnus?'

'Yes,' said Andrew Murray. 'He can draw, if nothing else!'

Magnus ran round behind the schoolhouse, away from the others, to examine the field-mouse in peace. 'Come out, you.' He lifted it from his pocket and held it gently in his hand, noting every detail of its whiskers, its tail, its small bright eyes. Yes, that was it! He had a complete picture of it in his mind. Now he could set it free. 'Away you go.'

The mouse sat still on the grass for a moment, not be-lieving its luck, then scuttled off, never to be seen again.

Ping!

A pebble whizzling through the air missed Magnus's head by inches. He whirled round to find the Ferret creeping up on him with his catapult at the ready. 'I'll shoot you, Magnus Macduff, for stealing my mouse!' he cried, red with rage.

'Away,' said Magnus, giving him a push. They tussled for a few moments, grunting like pigs – half in fun, half in earnest – and then gave it up. As a final insult, they stuck out their tongues at each other, and then went their ways. It was all part of their peculiar relationship. They would fight at the least provocation, but if either was in trouble, they would band together like brothers.

The District Nurse was coming out of the Cowans' cottage as Magnus ran home.

'She's worse,' she said cheerfully. Mrs Gillies thrived on other people's illness. 'Temperature's away up. I shouldn't be surprised if she's sickening for something. You'd better keep out of her way. You might catch it.'

'What? I thought it was only a chill.'

'Ah, you never know what might develop,' said Mrs Gillies hopefully.

The truth was, the islanders were too healthy for her liking. There was seldom a dose of 'flu let alone an epidemic. Even the mumps and the measles seemed to have by-passed Sula. It was enough to put her off her profession. After all her training! True, there was the time when the goat took whooping-cough and when Tair got his head stuck in the pail he was wearing as a helmet. But Mrs Gillies thought little of that. She was a Florence Nightingale at heart, and so far she had scarcely needed to light her lamp.

Magnus could hear sounds from the bedroom above the shop. Cough! cough! cough! Poor soul! He felt sorry for Jinty. She was a nuisance, of course, but a familiar nuisance, like Gran's aspidistra. The day was not the same without her. Maybe he would try to be nicer to her when she got better.

Gran was on her knees scrubbing the stone kitchen floor. It was clean enough already, but she had a few minutes to spare and was not going to waste them.

'Take your soup,' she said to Magnus, without looking up.

Magnus helped himself from the pot by the fire. It was Scotch broth – his favourite – full of barley, peas, turnip, leeks, and an odd lump of mutton here and there. Like the porridge, it put a good lining on the stomach. He ate it with a piece of barley-bannock, blowing on each spoonful to cool it. His fingers were itching for a pencil and a piece of paper on which to draw the field-mouse while it was fresh in his mind, but not with Gran watching.

There was no conversation between the two, but they were used to each other's silences. Gran gave a groan and a grunt as she rose to fetch a fresh pail of water, but that was the only sound, apart from the ticking of the grandfather clock.

The boy noticed that the pancakes had disappeared. He suspected that Gran had taken them to the teacher to share with the occupants of the painted yacht. Specky's egg lay on the table – he could tell it by its elongated shape – with a jam-jar full of soup, a lump of bannock and a large pat of butter. Gran packed the lot into a basket when she had finished washing the floor.

'Who's that for?' asked Magnus, wiping his plate clean with the last of his bannock.

'Him.' Gran always referred to the Hermit as *him*. 'Tell him, if he wants a job, he can dig the teacher's garden.'

Magnus was sure that Mr Skinnymalink would never come near the schoolhouse garden. Not unless he dug it at dead of night. All the same, he took the basket and set off. If he hurried he would be back in time to go to school in the afternoon. But would he bother? Yes! no! maybe!

He climbed up the Heathery Hill towards the cave and called 'Yoo-hoo!' when he reached the entrance. No reply! Not a sight nor a sound of the Hermit – only the charred remains of a fire, and a heap of coloured stones.

'He must have gone back to the hut,' thought Magnus,

scurrying down through the bracken. The Hermit changed his abode as the spirit moved him; but the hut, too, was empty. Where else could he be hiding?

Magnus began his game of hide-and seek, looking behind dykes, in broken-down barns, scanning the length and breadth of the island for a sight of the gaunt figure.

The Reverend Alexander Morrison was coming out of the Manse gate as he passed.

'A-tisket, a-tasket, what's in the basket?' The minister could never resist his wee joke. Give him a false nose and a funny hat, and he would have done fine in a music-hall.

Magnus gave him a glower and said, 'Food.' What he really wanted to say was, 'Mind your own business.' But the minister was not as silly as he looked. He knew what Magnus was up to. He also knew where the Hermit was hiding.

'He's in the hen-house,' he told the boy, and went on his way whistling a hymn-tune in double-quick time.

Magnus stared after him. The hen-house! It was little more than a lean-to at the back of the churchyard, always empty – for the minister kept no hens – except when Specky chose to pay it an odd visit. What on earth was the Hermit doing there?

He was sitttng on the dusty floor with all his bags and bundles beside him. He seemed to have packed up every once of his meagre possessions, except for the handful of stones he had left behind in the cave.

'What's up?' asked Magnus.

'Close the door!' The Hermit rose up to shut it him-self, after taking a furtive look outside. 'I'm going away.'

'Away?' Magnus looked stunned. He could not imagine Sula without the Hermit. He was part of the land-scape – as everlasting as a stone dyke. 'Going away?' He could not take it in.

'Too many people.'

That was the only explanation Mr Skinnymalink gave; but it was enough for Magnus. The yacht, that was it. The Hermit must have sensed what was afoot – strangers roaming all over the island with their inquisitive cameras.

'Where – where will you go?' asked the boy in a daze.

The Hermit jerked his thumb to the North-West.

'What?' gasped Magnus. 'Little Sula? But you can't live there!'

'Yes, I can.' There was a determined note in the Hermit's croaky voice. He had thought it all out. 'I can stay on the far side, out of sight, till that yacht goes away.'

Magnus still looked stunned at the thought of the Hermit living all alone on Little Sula, except for the black-faced sheep. What if a storm blew up? What if he fell ill? How would he find food?

Another startling thought struck him. 'How are you going to get across?'

Dark though it was in the hen-house, it was light enough for Magnus to see that the man had fixed him with his eye. No words required. The boy knew that *he* would have to row the Hermit across.

'When?' he asked, accepting his fate.

'Tonight. As soon as it's dark enough. You'll do it?'

Magnus nodded. Yes, he would do it. Never mind how difficult it would be getting out of the house without Gran knowing. Never mind anything. If the Hermit wanted to escape, *he* would help him.

Thinking of Gran, he remembered the message about the teacher's garden. No need mentioning it now. Indeed, there was nothing more to be said. Certainly nothing more that the Hermit wanted to say. He accepted the contents from the basket without a word, and sank back into silence. Magnus knew there was no use lingering. The bargain had been made, and they would both stick to their word.

As Magnus ran home with the empty basket, he heard the ringing of the school-bell. He hesitated for a moment. If he stayed away, would the teacher think he was afraid of the hangman's whip? He would go.

The man Jeremy and the blonde girl were wandering about in the weedy garden. 'There's the boy,' he heard the girl say, as he hurried towards the school door. The man turned and called to him: 'Hi! Wait a moment! I want to speak to you...' but Magnus darted into the schoolroom, pretending not to hear.

There was no sign of the hangman's whip. The episode seemed to be closed. Andrew Murray had a flushed look on his face. The result of meeting his friends from the yacht? At intervals he looked out of the window – to admire the scenery, or to catch a glimpse of the blonde girl?

He tried to pull himself together and make up for lost time, taking each pupil in turn for a private lesson, Magnus last of all. The boy occupied his time in drawing the field-mouse – every whisker in place – on the margin of his reading-book, not hearing the babble of sound around him.

Tair was learning a new piece of poetry: *Faster than fairies, faster than witches*. The Ferret was struggling with subtraction. One of the girls – Mirren – was trying to find Calcutta on the dusty globe, whirling it round and round and missing India every time. Black Sandy was fighting the Wars of the Roses – a losing battle – glowering now and then at Red Sandy who had been given the envied task of cleaning the blackboard.

Everything was going on at the same time: reading, history, geography, sums, but all of it washed over Magnus's head. If he was thinking of anything at all, it was about his midnight journey to Little Sula.

Andrew Murray came to him at last. 'May I sit down beside you, Magnus?' His leg was hurting and he stifled a sigh as Magnus moved along to make room for him. It was a tight squeeze. The boy felt trapped, sitting there so close to the schoolmaster.

The teacher noticed the drawing of the field-mouse but said nothing. He had picked up Magnus's pencil as if he, too, was itching to draw. The picture he had in his mind, however, was not of a field-mouse but of a girl with corn-coloured hair.

His reverie was broken by the Ferret turning round to ask him: 'Please, sir, how do you take away nothing from nothing?'

'What? Don't be so silly!' The teacher lent over, corrected the sum, and then turned to Magnus. 'Now then, what's it to be?'

Magnus gave him one of his looks. What did the man mean – what's it to be?

'Come on! I'm giving you a choice. What do you want to learn? Writing, arithmetic, geography, history? Or would you rather get on with your reading?'

Magnus was about to say 'Uh-huh' but changed his mind and gave a half-nod instead.

'Right! You get on with it by yourself. If you stick at the difficult words, let me know and I'll tell you.'

Not a word about the morning's rumpus. Magnus was surprised at the man's reasonable tone. The teacher, for a change, was treating him like a human being, not a backward infant. Okay! He would have a shot at the reading. What had he to lose?

The truth was, Andrew Murray was trying out a new type of strategy. It was the girl, Diana, who had suggested it. They had been discussing the boy in the schoolhouse over lunch provided by Gran – fresh herrings coated in oatmeal and fried in butter, followed by home-made pancakes and jam.

'I sympathize with that boy, and with you, too, of course, Andrew. *I* know! I used to be the same myself, always kicking against authority and hating everybody who tried to take away my freedom.' (As if *she* could ever have been anything but perfect, thought her host, watching her animated face as she spoke.) 'Better to leave him alone than try to push him. He'll find his own feet...'

'Silly young savage!' said Jeremy, who had no use for such finesse. 'What he needs is a good hiding.'

'No!' said the girl fiercely.

'All right; I'll try,' said Andrew, breaking up the argument.

He was both amazed and amused to see that it was already paying dividends. Magnus had settled down in a world of his own, and was following *Treasure Island* with his finger, mouthing the words to himself as he went along each line. Perhaps Diana was right – the boy would find his own feet.

The grandfather clock in the kitchen began to wheeze, ready to strike the hour. Twelve. Magnus crouched at

the window of the little upstairs
bedroom. He could see the dim
outline of a figure sitting at the
landing-stage near Gran's boat,
so immovable that he might have
been a rock or a piece of driftwood. It was the Hermit waiting
to be ferried across to Little Sula. Right! The time had
come.

He grabbed the paper-bag in which he had stowed
some left-overs from his supper – anything he could pick
up behind Gran's back to swell Mr Skinnymalink's
meagre supplies – a scone, an oatcake, an apple, a lump
of cheese. This was what worried the boy most – the lack
of food on the Hermit's hiding-place. There were no
vegetables and no berries on Little Sula. How would the
man survive?

But now the most pressing problem was how to get
down the creaky stairs without waking Gran. She slept in
the box-bed in the kitchen, an uneasy sleeper at the best
of times. The rustle of a mouse was enough to wake her.
How, then, was Magnus to get out of the house un-
heard?

It was the aeroplane that saved him. Every night, just
after twelve, it came droning over Sula, flying low and
buzzing like an over-loaded bumble-bee. Magnus took
the chance and made his exit under cover of the noise.
He could hear Gran stirring, turning over, and settling
down again. The unexpected squeak of a mouse might
wake her, but she was accustomed to the hum and drone
of the big bumble-bee.

The whole island was in darkness, except for one lit
window. Jinty Cowan's. Magnus had a guilty feeling

when he heard the faint sound of coughing. He had meant to visit her after school, but Gran kept him on the move. 'Mag-nus! Dig up some potatoes!' 'Mag-nus! Fetch in the cow!' 'Mag-nus! Nail up that fence!' 'Mag-nus . . .'

In his spare moments he had been studying *Treasure Island* which he had brought home from school and smuggled up to his bedroom. It was less strange to him now, with field-mice, seals, and puffins scattered throughout its pages. He was even beginning to get the hang of the story, though there were many words which puzzled him. Still, he was making progress. If the teacher asked him to read aloud, he would have a shot at it. As for Jinty, he would go and visit her, first thing in the morning.

The Hermit heard him coming and rose to help with the boat. No words were spoken. Action was more important than conversation. Each took an oar and pulled swiftly from the shore, rowing steadily – stroke for stroke – as if they had been training together for weeks.

The glow in Jinty's window went out. Now there was only the moon and the light from the painted yacht to guide them. No other sign of life on the sea. The fishing-boats were far out beyond the harbour-wall on their way to search for bigger fish in deeper water.

The Hermit seemed anxious to put as much distance as possible between himself and the yacht.

'Round the other side, quick,' he said, dipping his oar into the water with an even faster stroke.

Magnus suddenly had a feeling of high adventure – like *Treasure Island* – or as if he was helping Bonnie Prince Charlie to escape, though Mr Skinnymalink, with his matted hair and ragged clothes hardly fitted the romantic role. As they rounded the island they heard sleepy sounds of protest from the sea-birds and saw the sheep huddled together as if for protection. Was that a rabbit scuttling into its hole? Little Sula seemed alive with small movements and sounds.

It took only a few minutes to land the boat and carry the Hermit's belongings on shore. Magnus was reluctant to leave him.

'Will you be all right?'

'Of course.'

The Hermit looked happier already, now that he was out of sight of any human being. He had found a shelter – a small hollow in the rocky hillock on the far side of the island, with only the empty sea to spy on him.

'I'll come back as often as I can,' promised Magnus.

Mr Skinnymalink nodded. He held out his hand. 'Thanks, Magnus,' he said, and turned away.

The boy rowed home alone over the moonbeams in the water. As he neared the shore he saw something that made his heart stand still. A ghostly figure was standing by the landing-stage.

It was Jinty Cowan in her white nightdress.

Chapter 10

UPS AND DOWNS

THE DISTRICT NURSE was in her element.

'Pneumonia, as near as nothing!' she said triumphantly, as she left the Cowans' cottage next morning. 'She must have caught another chill last night. The poor thing's been rambling.'

'Rambling?' said Magnus in alarm. He was kicking his heels at the door, heavy-eyed after his night's adventures; terrified, too, that Jinty had not only caught her death of cold, but had given the show away.

'Rambling in her head,' said Mrs Gillies, cheerfully. 'She's wandering. Chattering a lot of nonsense.'

'What about?' asked Magnus fearfully.

Mrs Gillies grasped her bicycle which she had left propped against the wall. It was a man's bicycle with a high cross-bar. 'The usual rubbish!' she said, standing on one leg like a clumsy ballet-dancer and trying to manoeuvre the other over the bar. 'Can't make head or tail of it! She mentions *you* a lot, Magnus. Upsidaisy! I'm away!'

'Wait, Mrs Gillies!' Magnus went running after her. 'She's not – not going to die, is she?'

The bicycle wobbled. 'Die? Oh no!' That was going a bit far, even for the District Nurse. 'But it'll be a long time before she's herself again,' she added brightly, and rode off ringing her bell to scatter the cocks and hens out of her path.

Magnus sighed with relief and went to lean against the wall where the bicycle had stood a few moments before. He was trying to summon up enough courage to go in and ask for the invalid. It was not his fault, but he could not help feeling responsible for her.

He thought back to last night. What a job it had been getting Jinty home! He was not sure whether she was awake or asleep, or how long she had been down by the shore. Certainly she was shivering with cold. He had taken off his jacket and wrapped it round her, half-carrying, half-dragging her back to the house.

The Cowans were sound asleep in their beds, snoring in different keys as he took her upstairs. There was a silly-looking crinoline-doll lying on her bed. Magnus tossed it on to the floor and helped Jinty in, tucking the clothes round her. She had muttered something, and then fallen into a feverish sleep, leaving him wondering whether to waken her mother or steal away, keeping it a secret.

103

In the end his courage failed him. He had gone away without saying a word; but there had been little sleep for him that night. What with thinking about Mr Skinnymalink alone on Little Sula, and Jinty tossing and turning in her bed, his mind was all topsy-turvy. The world was becoming too much for him. What he longed for most was to be left in peace with old Whiskers.

He could hear Mrs Cowan in the shop, talking away into the telephone to an unknown Somebody across on the mainland. She was giving her weekly order to be brought by the *Hebridean*. 'Yes, that's the lot. No, I'm wrong. Better send half-a-dozen tins of peaches. Our Jinty's partial to them. No, I'm sorry to say she's not too well. A chill. She's off her food. Oh yes, I expect she'll be all right. I'm keeping her in bed for a day or two. And how's everything with you?'

No use waiting till she stopped. Magnus knew she would go on for ages, saying the same things over and over again. He braved himself and decided to go upstairs and see Jinty for himself. He had a present for her in his pocket. It was nothing; only a wee minding. He would never have dreamt of giving it to her if she hadn't been ill.

The crinoline-doll was lying on the pillow with Jinty popped up beside it. The invalid's eyes were open, but there was a glazed look in them, as if she was half-asleep or away in another world. She looked at Magnus but did not seem to recognize him.

'He's away in a boat,' she said in a sing-song voice. 'Away over to Little Sula. I'm going to wait here till he comes back.'

'I'm here!' said Magnus, standing uncertainly at the

foot of the bed. 'I've – er – brought something for you, Jinty. A wee present.'

'A wee present!' repeated Jinty. She did not seem to believe he was really there. It was all part of a confused dream.

'Look.' He took it out of his pocket – a small spray of birds' feathers. He had found them lying on the Heathery Hill and liked their softness and subtle colours. He had taken them home to make a drawing, then smoothed them out and fastened them together. Jinty might wear them as a brooch, or on her Sunday hat, or do anything she liked with them. They were all he had to offer.

'Nice,' she said, picking them up and feeling their softness. Then her gaze wandered restlessly round the room. 'Do you know where Magnus is?'

'I'm here! Can you not see me?' He spoke sharply, in the voice he normally used when talking to Jinty. He was getting fed-up with her and her faraway voice and her crinoline-doll. He wanted to get out into the fresh air, away from the sick-room with its pink eiderdown and airy-fairy curtains. 'Stop being so silly!'

That did it. Jinty blinked her eyes, as if suddenly recognizing her master's voice. She gave a self-satisfied little smile when she saw him standing there and cried, 'Oh Magnus! Fancy you coming to see me! I was just thinking about you.' She looked at the feathers and held them to her flushed cheeks. 'Aren't they nice? It's a lovely present.'

'Away!' said Magnus, looking down at his feet. 'It's nothing.'

Suddenly the puzzled look came back into her eyes. 'I

was wondering,' she began; 'did I not meet you last night, Magnus?'

'Where?' Magnus gave her a quick look.

'Where?' Jinty tried to sort out her thoughts. 'I don't know where. At the boat, I think.' She sighed. 'Maybe it was just a dream.'

'Ay, maybe it was,' said Magnus hastily, thankful to realize that she didn't *really* remember. 'Here! You'd better have a wee sleep.'

'Okay.' She pushed the doll off the pillow and laid the feathers in its place. 'You'll come back and see me again, Magnus?'

'Maybe.'

'That'll be nice.' She snuggled her head on the pillow, closed her eyes, and began to breathe deeply and evenly.

'Come here, boy!'

They were out filming – the man Jeremy and the girl with the blonde hair – roaming all over the island taking what they called 'random shots'. Magnus tried to keep out of their way. Let them get on with it! There were plenty of others willing enough to get into the picture, including the Reverend Alexander Morrison. With his deer-stalker hat stuck at a jaunty angle he came walking straight towards the camera, showing every one of his false teeth in a broad smile. A perfect picture – so he thought – of a Sporting Parson. The Ferret darted here and there, turning self-conscious somersaults to attract the film-makers. Tair kicked a football in front of them. Even old Bilko, the goat, seemed to be striking a pose; and the seagulls sitting on the harbour wall were preening their feathers.

The man and the girl were calling to Magnus, trying

to get him to climb the Heathery Hill. 'Do come along,'
said the girl in a wheedling voice. 'All we want you to do
is be yourself. Act naturally. Run about. Climb the Hill.
Pull some flowers...'

She might as well have spoken to the wind. Magnus
made off at high speed in the opposite direction, running
half-doubled, as if that would make him invisible. *He*
was no puppet on a string, to prance at their bidding.
'Go away! Leave me in peace!' he kept shouting within
himself.

At last – well out of their reach – he came to his
favourite spot, the rock jutting out over the water. No
one in sight. He scrambled across and flung himself
down. This was it. Sun. Sea. Peace. All he needed now
was his old companion.

'Come on, Whiskers! It's me!'

He pulled the whistle from his pocket and played
softly, up the scales and down again. Now and then he
tried a shaky tune, full of discords. *Speed, bonnie boat.*

A questing head popped out of the water. Old
Whiskers took a cautious look round, then gave a grunt,

as if to say, 'Thank goodness, it's you at last. Where on earth have you been?'

Magnus made room for him as the seal slithered up on to the rock. They sat for a while side-by-side till the sun's rays dried the drops of sea-water from old Whisker's body. Then they both sighed with satisfaction and snuggled down together. The boy flung his arm across the seal's body and – united – they drifted off to sleep.

In the boy's case, it was a deeper sleep than usual, worn out after last night's adventures. Through it all he was conscious of a feeling of well-being: the sun warming his body, the seal lying grunting at his side, the lullaby of the lapping waves, the call of the sea-birds. He was in a kind of limbo, far away from the world's troubles and the people who caused them.

Not for long. It was old Whiskers who woke him. The seal gave a sudden squeal of alarm, shuffled off the rock, and splashed into the sea. Magnus sat up, rubbing his eyes, and turned round to find himself face-to-face with a whirring camera.

'Splendid! Just what we wanted! The boy and the seal. That'll take a trick.' The man, Jeremy, had an exultant note in his voice, but the blonde girl looked uneasy when she saw the fury blazing from Magnus's eyes.

'I say, I'm sorry, Magnus. We really ought not to have...' she began, then stopped suddenly when she saw the look of contempt in his gaze. For a moment he thought of diving at the man, wrenching the camera from him and throwing it out into the sea. Instead, without a word, he ducked down and rushed past them, zig-zagging away like a hounded hare. His face, even under the sunburn and freckles, was white with rage. He longed to hit out at someone with his fists. If only the

Ferret had been within sight, he would have knocked him down, for no other reason than to get rid of his fury.

Where could he go to escape his tormentors? His first impulse was to take Gran's boat and row across to Little Sula to hide there with the Hermit. But *they* would be sure to see him. 'What a wonderful shot! The boy rowing across to that little island. Let's follow him!'

He ran home instead. Luckily Gran was out. There was no one in the house except Specky pecking for crumbs on the kitchen floor; no one to stop him as he stumbled up the steep stairs and flung himself face-down on the bed.

There was a hot feeling at the back of his eyes and a tightness in his throat. He was not going to cry! No! not even here, in his own room, with no one to see. He hit the pillow with his fists, for want of anything better, and presently lay still, shutting his eyes to keep back the tears.

Once more he fell asleep, but it was not the same as it had been on the rock. This was an uneasy sleep, with many tossings, turnings, and strange dreams. He was about to fall over a precipice when he jerked himself awake. Saved at the last moment!

What was that? A step on the stair. Not Gran's. This was lighter and brisker.

'Are you there, Magnus? May I come in?' It was the young woman, Diana. 'There was no one about, so I just walked in. I hope you don't mind.'

Hot and flushed, Magnus sat up and stared at her. Was there no escape, not even in the privacy of his own small bedroom?

'I had to come and see you,' she said, sitting down on the small hard chair by his bedside. 'About those pic-

tures. It's all right; I've made Jeremy promise he won't use them without your permission. It was unfair of us. Believe me, Magnus, I know how you feel. You're so like what I used to be.'

'What?'

Magnus had not been listening to her before, but now his attention was captured. How could *he* have anything in common with *her*?

'Oh yes! We're alike in many ways, Magnus, except that I hadn't your advantages when I was a child – the advantages of living in this lovely remote island.'

She gazed out of the window, harking back in her thoughts to her own stormy childhood, with all its failures and frustrations, remembering her fight against authority, and her fierce determination to achieve independence.

'Like you, Magnus, I wanted freedom more than anything. Freedom to go my own way, and not to be swallowed up by the crowd. But I lived in the city, where it was not easy to be an individual. There were too many people pushing and pulling, trying to make me go their way.' The old anger came back into her voice as she spoke. 'How would you like to be sent to boarding-school? Never to be alone. Sleeping in a dormitory. Conforming to a set of rigid rules . . .'

Magnus listened as she went on, seeing something of himself in that rebellious schoolgirl, forgetting his own bitterness now that he could share it with someone.

'But we all find ourselves in the end,' she said, sitting up straighter and shaking off the past. 'I just wanted to come and say I'm sorry. Are we friends, Magnus?'

'Uh-huh.'

It was not an insolent 'Uh-huh'. The girl recognized it for what it was – a peace pact – and gave him a bright smile as she rose to go. She took a quick look out of the window at a solitary figure limping along the sands with a small dog dancing at his heels. 'He's out of step, too,' she sighed, turning to Magnus. 'The schoolmaster. I wish you would help him, Magnus.'

'What? Me? Help the schoolmaster?'

'Poor man! he's very lonely and unsure of himself.' A warmer note crept into her voice as she spoke of him. 'Think what it must be like to have his disability. He's trying so hard to find his feet, in more ways than one; but he needs help.'

She said no more, but her eyes, meeting Magnus's, were asking a question. 'Won't *you* help?'

He looked back at her, a straight glance, which could be interpreted as, 'I might.'

'Mag-nus!'

'Yes, Gran.'

'You'd better go and have a look at the sheep.'

It was next day – a day spent caged in the schoolroom, trying his best to conform. The teacher, too, seemed anxious to avoid clashes, and left him to his own devices, after suggesting that he might write an essay on My Favourite Hobby.

What on earth was a *hobby*? Magnus licked his pencil and gazed at his blank jotter. At the end of the day there were few words written down. Instead, crabs, crocodiles and prehistoric animals crept and crawled across the page. Perhaps they were his hobby!

At home, he looked uneasily at Gran and asked, 'What sheep? Where?'

She shot him a keen glance. 'You know where! Little Sula, of course! Here you'd better take this parcel with you.'

'What's in it, Gran?'

'Food.' She turned away so that their eyes could not meet.

'Oh! Thanks, Gran.'

She knew! Gran was no fool. She had always been better than most folk at putting two and two together. Better, too, at keeping her own counsel. His secret – and the Hermit's – was safe with her.

'You'd better go now,' she said, rolling up her sleeves, ready for the next household task. '*They*'re away back to the yacht.'

They had been following her about all day with their inquisitive cameras. Gran was no film-star, with her weather-beaten face and outlandish garments, and had as little desire as Magnus to appear on any screen. Yet, *she* could not run away, as he had done. Her work must go on. She had to dig peat, hang out the washing, do the milking, and gather the eggs, no matter who was watching. As often as she could, she turned her back on them, and went stramping about in her big boots, with a grim expression on her face.

When Magnus was ready to go she went to the dark cupboard in the hallway – the *press*, she called it – and took out an old set of oilskins which the boy had not seen before. His heart began to thump unsteadily. Were they his father's? Perhaps he had been wearing them that stormy night when his boat had gone down off Sula Point.

One look at Gran's face and he knew he could not ask any questions. 'Take them!' she said, thrusting them at Magnus. '*He'll* maybe need them.'

'Right, Gran!'

It was a strange feeling, rowing across to Little Sula in the gloaming with the oilskins lying in the boat; almost as if his father was there with him. How often *he* must have rowed in this same boat. Had he been a rebel, too? There must be some link between them, other than a set of mildewed garments.

Magnus gave an owl-call as he edged the boat round to the far side of the island. The sea-birds rose screeching into the air in angry protest. The black-faced sheep raised their heds and stared stupidly at him as he beached the boat and called out: 'All clear! It's only me!'

He heard the Hermit long before he saw him. Mr Skinnymalink was coughing, a hard deep cough, which would have delighted the District Nurse, but which alarmed Magnus so much that he ran pell-mell towards the rocky hollow where the man was sheltering. What if he turned ill, alone here with no one to help him?

'Are you all right?' he called out anxiously.

'Yes,' said the Hermit; and indeed – to Magnus's relief – he seemed the same as ever, though he was chittering with cold. The night air on Little Sula was chill, and he had not dared, for caution's sake, to light a fire at which he could have warmed himself and brewed a hot drink.

'Here! Put them on.' Magnus helped him into the oilskins. They hung loosely from his shoulders, making him look even more like a scarecrow. 'I've brought some food from Gran. She guessed.'

'Who else?' Mr Skinnymalink shot him a sharp glance. 'Not them? From the yacht?'

Magnus shook his head. 'No! No one else knows; and they'll be going away soon.'

'Good.' The Hermit gathered the oilskins round him and crouched back into his cramped quarters, giving way to another fit of coughing. Magnus noticed that he had already collected a small heap of coloured stones to polish. If only he could have the comfort of a fire, he would come to little harm during his exile.

He had retreated into one of his long silences. Magnus might not have been there for all the notice he took of him. Yet the boy knew that this withdrawal – like that of old Whiskers – hid a deep and abiding companionship. Words were not needed.

He opened Gran's parcel and found buttered scones, ham sandwiches, hard-boiled eggs, and – Gran thought of everything! – a small packet of tobacco. At the sight of it, the Hermit's eyes brightened. He fumbled in his pocket and brought out his battered pipe. Soon he was puffing and coughing, and trying with each puff to wave away the smoke so that it might not be seen from a distance.

What was he hiding from, Magnus wondered? *Them*, like enough! Was it the young man or the blonde girl? What did it matter? Let everyone keep their own secrets.

The boy left him to take a quick look at the sheep. They were chewing non-stop at the fresh sweet grass; and already seemed to have put on weight from their change of diet. 'You'll sink the boat on the way back!' he said, thumping Blackie's woolly coat as she stood in the centre of the Fairy Ring, looking up at him with vacant eyes. He must draw a picture of her like that, with the other sheep – like ladies-in-waiting – assembled around her. 'Here move over and let me in.'

Magnus made a quick wish, not for himself, but for Mr Skinnymalink. 'Keep an eye on him, please!' he beseeched the Unknown. He had a feeling that the Hermit would need help, supernatural or otherwise, before long.

He had eaten one of Gran's sandwiches and drunk the milk by the time Magnus returned. The boy knew from his expression that he had something to say.

'What's his name?'

'The man on the yacht? I don't know his last name, but they call him Jeremy,' said Magnus.

The Hermit gave a shiver – or was it a shudder? – and

pulled the oilskins up round his face, as if to hide himself from the world.

'He'll be away soon,' said Magnus, anxious to give him a word of comfort. He was loath to leave the man there in his lonely hide-out. 'I'll be back tomorrow,' he promised.

No response, except for a fit of coughing. Magnus felt uneasy as he went away back to the boat. Was there a link beteen the Hermit and the man Jeremy? Was it the same as the link between himself and the oilskins?

Chapter 11

A STORMY NIGHT

'HANDS UP ANYONE who can tell me who killed Goliath. And it's no use saying. "Please, sir, it wasn't me"!'

The Reverend Alexander Morrison was giving the class a Bible lesson, while Andrew Murray sat back watching and listening. It was difficult to hide his irritation when he saw that, even with such a subject, the minister must have his little joke.

The Ferret put his hand half-way up, then thought the better of it, and put it down again. He was hoping that Kirsty McLeod, sitting in front of him, might leap to her feet with the answer. He had fastened her long pigtail to his ink-well and was looking forward to some fun. It wasn't so easy to get fun nowadays in the classroom. If only the teacher wasn't sitting facing him, he could have bombarded His Reverence with pellets. *He* was a far better target than Goliath.

'Come on!' urged the minister. 'What a dumb lot you are! Surely somebody knows about Goliath.'

Tair suddenly shot up his hand, urged on by Avizandum in his pocket, whispering, 'Have a bash! Say anything that comes into your head!'

'Please, sir, Goliath was a man in the Bible!'

'A man, eh? You're sure he wasn't a mouse? What kind of a man?'

Tair considered for a moment, and then replied, 'A great muckle big man!'

'So he was! And who killed the great muckle big man?'

'A wee boy!'

'Right! And what was the name of the wee boy?'

Tair could not remember. Avizandum made a wild suggestion. 'Moses!' At least, it was a Bible name.

'Off-side!' said the minister, putting on his funny face. 'Try again.'

Following their usual custom of pulling the minister's leg, the class put forward various unlikely names. 'Hamish!' 'Geordie!' 'McTosh!' 'Ringo!' The suggestions grew wilder and wilder, until even Mr Morrison had had enough.

'No, no! You're all mixed up. Wait! I'll read you the whole story. Are you listening?'

'Yes, sir!'

The class settled down – more or less – to listen, except Magnus who let the words roll unheeded over his head. He drew a lion on the margin of his Bible. There were dozens of creatures there already, all inhabitants of the Ark. Two by two they crept across the Preface and crawled into Genesis and Exodus. But Magnus was not thinking of Noah, or anyone in the Bible. He was worrying about Mr Skinnymalink, alone on Little Sula.

'Have you been listening, Magnus?' His Reverence had finished the story and was now ready to ask questions.

'Uh-huh.'

'Good! Then get to your feet and tell me the whole story.'

Magnus shuffled to his feet with not a thought of Goliath in his head, except that he was somebody in the Bible. A giant who had killed a shepherd-boy. Or was it the other way round? He caught a look of sympathy from Andrew Murray. He certainly needed it.

He took a look at the ceiling, trying to find inspiration; then gazed out of the window. Suddenly his face brightened. Saved! The *Hebridean* was making her way towards the pier. The next moment three loud blasts from the siren could be heard, the signal for everyone on the island to down tools and rush to the harbour.

The Reverend Alexander Morrison was already making for the door, tucking his Bible into his coat-pocket, not even waiting to say goodbye to the class. All the children were on their feet – Kirsty tugging at her pigtail – ready to follow him, when the teacher called, 'Wait! Where do you think you're all going?'

Where? They paused on their way to the door to stare at him. Old Miss Macfarlane would never have asked such a daft question. Surely the man didn't expect them to do lessons when the *Hebridean* was in. It was an unwritten law that everybody stopped work, even Gran.

'Please, sir; it's the boat, sir.' The Ferret tried his best to explain. If only Jinty had been here, *she* would have acted as spokeswoman, but she was still off, feeling 'poorly'. No one else was able to state the case with her gift of the gab.

Avizandum had a word in Tair's ear. 'Tell him it's an old Sula custom!'

'What?' said Tair doubtfully. However, it was worth a

119

try. Up went his hand. 'Please, sir, it's an old Sula custom.'

'So I gather,' said the teacher, with a faint smile on his
lips. 'All the same, you might at least ask permission before you leave the classroom.'

Silence. The children looked at each other uneasily.
Who was going to ask? Magnus turned his head away.
The Ferret scuffled his feet. The rest stared at each
other, wondering who was going to frame the request.

It was left, as usual, to a lassie. Kirsty put up her hand
and spoke in a breathless lisp. 'Pleathe, thir, can we get
out?'

'All right! Off you go!'

'Oh, thank you, thir!'

They all dived for the door at the one time, shoving,
pushing, and bumping into each other. Once outside
they went helter-skeltering down to the harbour, whoop-
ing with high spirits. They were free! The boat was in!
This was the most exciting moment of the week!

The quiet harbour had suddenly wakened up and was
buzzing with activity. Men, women, children, dogs, cats,
hens – and Old Cowan's goat – had all assembled there,
eager to see all the comings and goings. Everyone was
present, except Jinty who leant limply from her window,
like a lady in a ballad, with a shawl over her white nightdress. She was not going to be left out entirely.

'Who's coming off?'

This was the first excitement – to see if any newcomer
would walk down the gangway – but today it was only
old Mrs McCallum, Tair's Granny, who had been across
on the mainland visiting her married daughter, and
thankful to get back, by the look of her.

'Oh my! It's great!' she kept saying, as her family

swarmed round her, helping to carry her parcels and suitcase. 'Great to be back home!'

The film-makers were there, too, having a high old time. No lack of random shots today! Crates of supplies for Cowans' shop came swinging through the air. Bundles of newspapers and mail landed with a thud on the cobbled quay-side. Captain Calum Campbell sauntered down the gangway to stretch his legs on shore. Fishboxes hung in mid-air. Excited sea-gulls dive-bombed into the water and flew off with crusts of bread in their beaks. Half-a-dozen sheep, destined for an unknown fate, refused to be driven on board, and who could blame them? But there was no escape. They were rounded up, and taken below deck where they stood huddled together, bleating piteously.

'Trix! Where's Trixie?' Andrew Murray was limping along the quay-side looking for his dog. 'She was here a moment ago. Where on earth can she have gone?'

She had gone on board with the sheep. It was Magnus who caught sight of her, almost swamped by her bleating companions. 'I'll go and fetch her,' he volunteered, and was off like a streak up the gangway. The teacher felt a pang of envy as he watched the lithe young figure moving with such swift grace. The cameras were watching, too, and when the boy returned with the dog in his arms, he glared at them angrily and dropped the dog at Andrew Murray's feet, before hurrying away out of reach.

But at least he had made a friendly gesture; and the teacher called after him, 'Thank you, Magnus!' with a note of real warmth in his voice.

Jinty waved a languid hand out of the window and called, 'Yoo-hoo! Magnus! Are you not coming up to see me?'

'No,' said Magnus gruffly. 'I can see you from here.' Not that he wanted to look at her. Why should he bother? She was getting better, wasn't she?

Jinty tried again. "I'm feeling fed up,' she said in a pathetic voice.

The truth was, she was no longer an object of interest, except to herself. Even the District Nurse had given her up. 'You're almost back to normal,' she had told her, not without a sigh of regret. 'Better stay in the house for a day or two; then back to school. That's another off my books. I've only got the minister's wife left, and all *she* has is heart-burn.'

Seeing Jinty at the window – a perfect target – the Ferret decided to take a pot-shot at her with his catapult; but Magnus tripped him up in time. The next moment they were in one of their rough-and-tumble clutches, with Jinty leaning out of the window, acting as referee in favour of Magnus.

'Let him have it, Magnus! Give him a black eye!' But their hearts were not in it. They could fight any day. Meantime there was too much going on at the harbour. After a few kicks and shoves they called a truce, turned their backs on the languid figure at the window, and ran down, side by side, to the harbour.

The Captain was smoking his pipe and talking to Gran about the weather. He had a great respect for her powers of forecasting, and would sooner consult her than any barometer.

'There'll be no fishing tonight,' she was telling him. 'Too risky for the boats to go out. There's a storm coming up.'

Magnus heard her with a feeling of excitement. Was it to be a real storm, or only one of the smaller gales that

ruffled the island from time to time? Some said that
Gran was over-cautious about the boats, but who could
blame her when her only son had perished on the rocks?
Better be safe than sorry.

'Well, we'll be back on the mainland before anything happens,' said Captain Campbell, knocking out
his pipe. 'You're not thinking of coming across for a
trip?'

It was one of his jokes, said with such regularity that
Gran hardly bothered to reply. He knew that wild horses
– far less the *Hebridean* – would never force her to leave
Sula, even for a day trip.

'Is that everything on board? Well, you'd better get
away,' she said briskly. She was not one to stand about
making small-talk.

There was a strange feeling of emptiness when the
ship slid away from the pier and waltzed round with a
final blast from the siren. Their only link with the outside world was broken. But there were compensations. A
queue began to form outside Cowans' shop. That night
there were letters and newspapers to read, and a high tea
on every table.

This was the one day in the week when imported
foods replaced the more homely fare. Sausages sizzled in
frying-pans. Baker's bread, rolls, and buns took the place
of home-baking. It was a hunger or a burst. Those who
could afford it had butcher-meat roasting in the oven;
and appetizing aromas issued from every cottage.

Even Gran, who did not believe in 'fancy rubbish',
had made some purchases. Magnus hurried into the
house, hoping for a treat, and was not disappointed. His
mouth began to water when he smelt the kippers frying,
and saw that there was a crusty loaf and a packet of

mixed biscuits on the table. It was no banquet, but any change of diet was welcome.

Gran poured out the tea from the brown earthenware teapot and cut thick slices from the loaf. Then she closed her eyes for a moment to say her own private grace. Magnus, too, shut his eyes, and opened them again quickly to examine the kipper on his plate before dissecting it with his knife and fork. He was extracting the backbone and admiring its symmetry when the first whiff of wind rattled the window-panes. He looked up at Gran enquiringly. Was this it? The storm?

She shook her head. It was only the preliminaries; enough to show that her forecast was right. After a few gusts, it died down again, but it was an uneasy calm that followed, as if a monster was saving his strength for a battle.

There was no lingering over the meal. Gran was on her feet before Magnus had picked his kipper clean. 'Better see that everything's safe,' she said, flinging her old jacket round her shoulders. 'If it gets worse, we'll need to take the sheep off Little Sula.' And not only the sheep. 'Hurry, Magnus!'

He ran first to the Heathery Hill to bring down the few sheep still grazing there. Then, to their surprise, he chased the hens into the hen-house. 'You, too, Specky. Come on.' She was reluctant to conform – a rebel like himself – and ran hither and yon playing catch-as-catch-can. Finally he pounced on her and swooped her up into his arms. 'Silly thing! In you go. You'll be safe there if the storm comes.'

He bolted the door and went off to round up Gran's cow. Mary-Ann looked at him in surprise. She had already been milked. What was all the fuss about? 'Come on, you!' He gave her a friendly push. 'You're going to sleep under cover tonight, whether you like it or not.'

Cowan's goat was wandering aimlessly about. 'Here! You'd better have a night's shelter, too, and no fighting with Mary-Ann,' said Magnus, tugging him into the byre.

The lull lasted so long that when Magnus went upstairs to bed he wondered if Gran had been wrong. Not a whisper of wind! Not a cloud scurrying across the night sky! Nothing suspicious to be seen, when he took a last look out of his bedroom window, except a huddle of seabirds down by the harbour. They were mewing at each other as if arguing where to hide when the storm broke. Would the inhabitants of Little Sula be safe till morning?

It was the scream of the wind that woke Magnus in the middle of the night. It thumped and thudded against the window, like a wild beast trying to force its way in. 'Open up! You can't escape from me! I'm going to devour you.'

Magnus was out of bed like a shot, pulling on his clothes and calling, 'Gran! It's started!' He ran downstairs to find her, but she was not in the house. The old box-bed in the kitchen was empty. Bed was no place for Gran on the night of a storm.

Magnus tugged open the door and had difficulty in shutting it again. The wind almost blew the breath from his body. It came in great gusts, whipping the water into white horses and dashing it against the harbour wall. Clouds raced across the sky, and fat blobs of rain came pouring down in torrents.

The whole island seemed to be in turmoil. Gates were banging; slates were spinning off the roofs, and a pail came rattling past Magnus as if running for its life. The rowan tree in the Manse garden came crashing to the ground, and fences toppled down, as if blown over by a giant.

Magnus ignored it all. He had only one thought in his mind. Mr Skinnymalink! Somehow or other he must get across to Little Sula to rescue the Hermit.

He tried to run down to the harbour, but the wind held him back. He had to lean against it with all his might to keep on his feet. Between gusts he ducked down his head and battled forward – and then he saw her! Gran! She was down at the shore, pushing her boat into the water.

'Where are you going, Gran?' He had to shout against the howl of the wind.

'Across there.'

'To Little Sula? Wait! I'll come with you.'

'No! You take Cowan's boat. I'll get the sheep, if you get *him*!'

'Right, Gran!'

It was exciting in spite of the danger. Gran's boat pitched and tossed in front of him, her strong arms striving to keep it on a steady course. Magnus followed as best he could, flailing the swirling water with his oars. In-out! In-out! Beyond the harbour wall the sea was bubbling like a kettle on the boil. Where had old Whiskers gone to find refuge, he wondered?

He could see lights appearing in the windows as the islanders were wakened by the gale. It was comforting to watch their friendly glow when he looked back. But there were no lights ahead, and nothing to guide them towards the storm-tossed little rock where the Hermit was marooned. What if they missed it in the darkness and

126

were swept out into the endless ocean?

It was Gran, of course, with her sound judgment, who found the way to the little inlet. She was ashore, tying up her boat, when Magnus landed with a thud, swept in on the crest of a wave. He tugged his boat to safety, and without a word being spoken, they set off together. The sheep were standing in the Fairy Ring, their backs hunched against the wind, too terrified to bleat. They did not move even when Gran came and examined them closely.

'They'll be all right,' she said briskly. 'Find him.'

Magnus ran to the little shelter calling, 'Mr Skinnymalink! Mr Skinnymalink!' but the wind whipped the words away into the night, and if there was any answer who could hear it? The boy's heart was in his mouth when he saw the heap of oilskins lying limply on the sodden ground. Was there anything inside them?

'Mr Skinnymalink!'

The oilskins stirred.

'Oh, thank goodness!' gasped Magnus. 'Are you all right?'

'Fine,' said the Hermit, in a hoarse voice; but his eyes were glazed and he wheezed when he spoke. Every breath seemed to hurt him.

'Gran! He's here!' called Magnus. 'How will we get him home?'

Another movement from the oilskins. 'No! I'm not leaving here!'

Gran came and knelt down beside him. From the depths of her pocket she brought out a small bottle, and put it to his lips. 'Drink this. Come on; it'll do you good.'

She forced some brandy into his mouth, and as he

127

gulped it down she said, 'You've got to leave here. It'll be all right. You'll be safe with us. No one will see you. Come along; another drink. That's better.'

As soon as he began to revive, they half-carried him to the boat, one of his arms flung around each of their shoulders. They were used to heavier burdens. The Hermit was so light, it was almost like carrying a rag-doll. The trouble was not his weight, but the force of the wind trying to fling them off their feet.

They left him in the boat and went to fetch the sheep. 'Come on, Blackie. Move!' cried Magnus, thumping her wet woolly back; but she seemed rooted to the spot. They had to push and prod and carry before they got them all down to the shore and safely into Gran's boat.

'We'll have to hurry,' she said, pushing off. 'The storm's gathering.'

The whole sea seemed to be boiling up beneath them. Magnus's arms ached as he kept a tight grip on the oars to prevent them from being whipped out of his hands, In-out! In-out! Keep it up, Magnus! Keep it up!

Sometimes the boat was swept sideways, or in a complete circle aiming back towards Little Sula. Sometimes he had to stop and bale out while his helpless passenger lay limply in the prow. Gran and he passed and re-passed each other, narrowly avoiding bumping together. There was nothing for it but to clench his teeth and keep at it – in-out! in-out – in the hope that somehow they would reach the shore.

Suddenly the boy let out a cry of alarm. 'Gran! Look! The yacht!'

The painted yacht had drifted from her moorings and was swaying first one way and then the other, as if trying to keep her balance in a drunken dance. Any moment, it

seemed, she would topple over and be lost for ever. What could they do to help, when they were fighting for their own lives?

'The lifeboat!' shouted Gran.

If she had been on shore she would have given the order to launch it; but luckily Cowan had seen the danger and used his own judgment for once. In a few moments they saw the boat bouncing over the waves, making straight for its target. The crew waved and shouted as they swept past; and Gran and Magnus were left to concentrate on their own salvation.

In-out! In-out! Both of them put on desperate spurts to reach the sheltering arms of the little harbour. They could sense rather than see dim figures moving about on shore, and felt a flood of relief to know that help was so near at hand.

Already some were wading into the water to meet them. Amongst them was one with a limp. It was Andrew Murray – weakling though he was – who reached Magnus first and grabbed the boat to prevent its being sucked back into the swirling sea. The boy leapt out, and together they tussled against the wind, while other helping hands brought Gran to safety.

Without waiting to ask questions, the schoolmaster helped to hoist the limp figure from the boat and carry him ashore.

'Wait! I'll help you,' cried the minister, hurrying to ease their burden. For once he had no joking remarks to make. 'I'll look after him. I know who he is.'

'So do I,' said the teacher, pushing him aside. 'I'll take him to the schoolhouse.'

Magnus stared at him. How could the teacher know anything about an outcast like Mr Skinnymalink?

Andrew Murray was chafing the Hermit's cold hands and wrapping the oilskins protectingly round the wet body. 'Don't worry!' he said soothingly. 'I'll take care of you, Uncle Andrew.'

Chapter 12

STEPPING-STONES TO
THE FUTURE

'PLEASE, SIR, Miss Macfarlane could play the piano with *two* hands,' said Jinty Cowan, always eager to impart information. She was back in her place at school, wearing her new feather-brooch, and ready as usual to speak up for the rest of the class.

'Could she, indeed,' said Andrew Murray mildly. There was a more relaxed look about him nowadays. He was finding it easier, it seemed, to keep his irritation under control. Otherwise, he would have been quick enough to tell Jinty what he thought of her. 'Well, I can only play with one finger,' – and not very well at that, if the truth were told.

He had just discovered that all-in education on Sula included a subject which, up till now, he had neglected. Singing! He had looked hastily through the tattered music on the school piano to find something suitable, and had discarded Miss Macfarlane's repertoire as hopeless. It consisted mainly of *Twinkle, twinkle, little star*, *Water, water, wallflower*, and *Here we go round the mulberry bush*. He was no musician, but he felt that the class deserved something better.

'Do you know the *Londonderry Air*?' he asked hopefully.

'No, sir; never heard of it.'

They were not really paying attention to him. They were too busy giggling at the Ferret who had been sent out to clean the blackboard. It was a great opportunity to draw funny faces and write such slogans as THE TEACHER'S A MUG. HIT HIM ON THE LUG. The Ferret, however, had no incentive powers. On the other hand, he was a born mimic.

After rubbing out the sums, he put the duster round his head, pulled a comical face – and suddenly became Gran. Another twist of the duster, another comical face – and he was the Reverend Alexander Morrison. On the way back to his seat, he did an imitation of the teacher, dragging one leg after the other in an exaggerated limp, dot-and-carry-one. The rest of the class sniggered, but for some reason Magnus felt himself beginning to boil with rage.

When the Ferret sank into his seat, well-pleased with his cleverness, Magnus hit him over the head with his ruler.

'What's that for?' asked the Ferret, swinging round in surprise.

'Because!'

'Because what?'

'Shut up!' hissed Magnus. 'I'll sort you later!'

'You will not!'

'I will so!'

This exchange of compliments might have ended in fisticuffs had not Andrew Murray called them to attention. 'Listen to this.'

He tried to pick out the *Londonderry Air* with one

finger on the yellow keys. Some were inclined to stick; others gave out tinny discords. Even so, the class recognized the tune.

'Please, sir, it's O Danny Boy,' said Jinty, getting in first.

'Right! Get on to your feet and sing it, the lot of you.'

'Please sir; don't know the words.'

'Make them up. Or just sing la-la. Are you ready? One-two...'

Never before had O Danny Boy sounded less like the *Londonderry Air*, and vice versa. The girls made a valiant effort and trilled away, more or less in tune, but the boys groaned and grunted several beats behind them. Tair, especially, had no ear for music, but he made up for it by singing louder than the rest in a high-pitched falsetto voice.

'You're sharp,' the teacher told him.

'Yes, sir,' said Tair, not sure whether it was a compliment or not.

'Don't you know your doh-ray-me's?'

'Sort of.'

'Sort of?' scoffed the teacher. 'What kind of answer is that?'

'Please, sir; I don't know, sir.'

'Well, think about it, and let me know when you've made up your mind!'

'Yes, sir.'

By now Tair did not know the question, let alone the answer. He had got along all right in old Miss Macfarlane's day with the Grand Old Duke of York. 'Watch it!' Avizandum warned him from his pocket. 'Say you've got a bad throat.'

'Please, sir, I've got a bad throat.'

'Fiddlesticks! There's nothing wrong with your throat. Keep on the tune. Let's try again. One, two . . .'

This time Avizandum gave him some sounder advice. 'Sing under your breath!' Tair mouthed his la-la's but made no sound, while the Ferret and Black Sandy began to make up their own words, with the odd giggle in between. 'O deary me! O deary, deary, deary me . . .'

As the lesson, such as it was, progressed, Andrew Murray took stock of himself. Here he was on a remote island far from the hub of world affairs, bending all his energies on a handful of restless children. Was it worth it? What did it matter to them whether they sang sharp or flat, or if they knew the capital of South America? Was he wasting his time?

No! He straightened himself up. His short stay on Sula was already showing results – in his own health, if nothing else. The plain food, the fresh air, the quiet days had benefited both his mind and his body. He was feeling calmer. He had put on weight. There were times when he felt the old surge within his veins, as if the future might hold a happy promise.

The brightest prospect of all was that Diana Maxwell might share that future with him. Nothing had been said. Yet they both knew, when she sailed away in the patched-up yacht, that their parting was not final.

'You'll come back, Diana?'

'Yes, Andrew; I'll come back!'

The singing was growing louder and the words stranger. Especially the Ferret's. 'Oh, hold your tongue! O hold your, hold your, hold your tongue . . .' Andrew Murray let it pass. He was still taking stock of himself, weighing up the pros and cons, and wondering if he was making any impact on any of the islanders.

Yes! He caught the direct glance of Magnus Macduff. It was a man-to-man look, without any criticism or contempt in it. Andrew Murray felt a warm glow of satisfaction. At long last he had made some progress in his relationship with this young rebel. Perhaps at last they were beginning to trust each other.

The break-through had come on the night of the storm, when so many strange things came to light. The strangest of all, to Magnus's mind, was about the Hermit. Mr Skinnymalink was not a nameless, homeless nobody. He was somebody. The teacher's uncle! The boy was astonished to find that fate had flung the two of them together on such an unlikely place as Sula, his own little island.

There had been no time to ask questions on the night of the storm. Indeed, many of them might never be answered. Why had Andrew Murray lost touch with his uncle in the first place? Did he suspect that the Hermit was hiding on the island? And why had Mr Skinnymalink run away from the world? Was the young man, Jeremy, from the yacht, his son? It was all as strange and unreal as a chapter from *Treasure Island*.

One thing was certain, the teacher was no coward in the face of danger. He had worked harder than any on that stormy night, helping to clear up the wreckage and lending a hand where it was most needed. His first duty, of course had been to preserve his uncle's privacy. It had not been easy to persuade the Hermit to be carried to the schoolhouse.

Though he was only half-conscious, he struggled to free himself. 'No, no! Leave me alone! I don't want anybody . . .' but in the end, he was too weak to fight for his freedom.

If there was one person who enjoyed the storm and its aftermath, it was the District Nurse. Mrs Gillies had always fancied herself in the role of Florence Nightingale, and here she was rushing from one sick-bed to another like a ministering angel. The exhausted occupants of the yacht had found refuge in the Manse. A few days of rest and they would be ready to sail away; but the Hermit would keep her busy for weeks. He needed injections and some of her special pills and potions, as well as long careful nursing before *he* would be on his feet again.

'It'll take weeks,' she gloated. 'Weeks! If not months.'

There were other minor ailments, too, to keep her happy. The Ferret was going about with an important-looking bandage round his head, hiding a cut from a flying slate. Old Mrs McLeod had a gash in her leg caused by stumbling over a broken fence in the darkness. 'It's an ill wind,' said Mrs Gillies, leaping on to her bicycle as if it were a charger. 'Thank goodness, I'm fully-stretched for once.'

Her most difficult patient by far was the Hermit who hid under the blankets when he heard her bouncing up the schoolhouse stairs, calling: 'And how are we today? Still very weak? Never mind, I've got some lovely medicine for you. Come along, now! This is no time to play peek-a-bo . . .'

My Skinnymalink had no desire to be treated like a naughty child – indeed, no desire to be treated at all. All he wanted was to be left alone. It was bad enough being hemmed in by four walls. When he first woke up and found himself in bed, with sheets and blankets tucked round him, he struggled to free himself. 'Let me out! Give me air!' he gasped.

Andrew Murray was there by his bedside, soothing

him. 'It's all right, Uncle. You'll soon be well, and then you'll get plenty of air. Lie still and rest.'

According to the District Nurse, it was sustaining food he needed, as much as rest. 'He's just a rickle of bones,' she declared. 'A skeleton has more flesh on him. He'll fade away.'

But Mr Skinnymalink was tougher than she thought. Every day he gained in strength and weight. His face lost its gaunt look, and soon he was able to sit up in bed and sup some of Gran's cocky-leekie soup. She came every day, but, unlike Mrs Gillies, did not intrude on his privacy.

'This is for *him*,' she would tell Andrew Murray, dumping a bowl or a basket on the table. 'There'll be enough for you, too, Mr Murray. All you need to do is heat it up.'

'You're a marvel, Mrs Macduff!' he said gratefully. 'I don't know how we'd ever survive without you.'

'Huh!' Gran had no time for compliments. 'If *he* needs anything else, tell the boy and he'll fetch it.'

Magnus was ready and willing to act as go-between. It was strange to tip-toe up the schoolhouse stairs and find the Hermit sitting up in bed wearing a pair of striped pyjamas. He seemed out of place in such surroundings. Yet he was the same Mr Skinnymalink, as silent as ever, except to say, 'Keep the door shut. Don't let that nurse-body in.'

He asked no questions about the yacht or the storm, or about Jeremy and the blonde girl. He seemed to have withdrawn from life once more, content for the moment to stare out of the window at the sky and the seagulls. But there was a look in his eyes which told that he was only biding his time.

The day came when he refused to stay in bed any

longer, but got up and began to wander round the room like a caged animal. Andrew Murray realized that the future must be faced. The yacht had gone; the coast was clear; would his uncle consent to stay on with him? Or would he insist on returning to his old furtive habits of hiding away in odd corners?

'What about it, Uncle?' he asked eagerly. As a small boy he had been fond of this strange man, and had grown fonder of him during the last few weeks of close contact. 'Why not stay here with me? There's heaps of room, and no one would trouble you here.'

The Hermit paced restlessly up and down. He said neither Yes nor No; and his nephew had enough sense not to press the point. Let him come and go as he liked. The door would always be unlocked; there would always be a meal and a bed for him. But no ties; no hard and fast rules.

It was left at that. For a time Mr Skinnymalink disappeared. He had gone back to his hovel at the far side of the island and taken up his old way of life. He spent hours on the Heathery Hill collecting coloured stones; hours sitting polishing them; hours when he would not utter a word, even to Magnus when he came to bring him food. He seemed to want to get back – away from human contact – to his old lonely ways.

Then gradually he came out of his shell. He was seen working on Gran's croft, or mending the Manse wall which had been blown down by the gale. More often he wandered into the schoolhouse garden and began the task of reducing the wilderness to some semblance of order.

There were nights when, having finished his work, he came into the house to share his nephew's supper. Afterwards the two of them would sit silently smoking. Then

Andrew Murray would say, 'The bed's there, Uncle. Better stay the night.'

Gradually it became a more regular habit, though the young man had enough sense not to urge his uncle to stay if he took one of his restless fits and showed signs of wandering off into the darkness. No ties; no hard and fast rules.

One evening they were sitting together after supper. The Hermit was quietly polishing one of his stones. Andrew Murray looked up from his book, catching a glint of coloured light, and said, 'You know, you could do something with these stones, if you liked, Uncle. They could be made into jewellery. If you sent them away to the mainland . . .'

The Hermit dropped the stone and looked up in alarm at the prospect of becoming involved in any kind of business deal. Nevertheless, as time went by he began to collect his hidden hoards and bring them to the schoolhouse. That was as far as he was prepared to go. It was left to his nephew to take the next step.

What to do? Andrew Murray stared thoughtfully at the heap of glowing colours. Perhaps he could consult Captain Campbell the next time the *Hebridean* came in. Who could tell? The small stones of Sula might yield an unexpected harvest in days to come.

The teacher's reverie was broken when the music petered out on a ragged note. He looked up and caught Magnus's gaze once more.

'Have you got a favourite tune?' he asked the boy.

'No!'

It was a definite No but not a defiant one.

'Please, sir; I have!'

It was Jinty, getting her tongue in again.

'All right.' The teacher gave a patient sigh. 'What is it?'

Jinty smiled her smug little smile, and told him. 'Just a song at twilight,' she said in a sickly-sweet voice.

'Away!' scoffed the Ferret, glowering at her. 'We're not going to sing *that*!'

For once Magnus agreed with him, and gave him a pat on the back instead of a thump. At that moment his attention was distracted by the sight of a gaunt figure passing by the window. It was Mr Skinnymalink, coming to work on the neglected garden. How wonderful to be a hermit, free to come and go, with no silly singing-lessons to worry him!

Andrew Murray noted his caged look and decided to give up the struggle. 'Right,' he said, closing the piano-lid. 'That's enough for one day. You can get away early.'

'Thank the Lord!'

It was Avizandum who had spoken out loud, though the words came through Tair's mouth.

'*What* did you say?' asked the teacher in a menacing tone.

'N-Nothing, sir.' Tair looked up at him so innocently that he decided to let it pass.

'Off you go! But be sure to be in your places in good time tomorrow morning.'

'Oh yes, sir. Cheerio, sir.'

Magnus, hemmed in by the others, was the last to shuffle to the door. The teacher was putting away the hangman's whip in his desk when he caught sight of a piece of paper on which was written in shaky letters: MY FAVOURITE HOBBIE. Magnus's essay! It was not the words – there were few enough of them – that

141

attracted his notice, but the crabs and crocodiles crawling across the page.

'Magnus!' he called out. 'Wait! Can you spare a moment?'

'Uh-huh.'

He came, though reluctantly, and stood at the desk, waiting. A flush came over his face when he saw his scraggly handwriting. The spelling was all wrong. Was the teacher going to keep him in and order him to rewrite the stupid thing?

Andrew Murray was not ordering; he was asking. 'Will you do me a favour, Magnus? I'd like you to draw some pictures for me. You know the kind – birds and beasts . . .'

Magnus knew the kind. But what was the man up to?

'I want to show them to an artist friend of mine. He'll be coming to visit me later on. Who knows? Perhaps he may be able to help you with your career.'

Career? The boy stared at him blankly. What career? *He* had no desire to gain honours and degrees, or to go out into the competitive world of big business. All he wanted was to stay on Sula and keep his freedom.

'You can't hide your talents for ever, Magnus,' said the teacher, guessing the thoughts that were passing through the boy's head. 'You have a great gift which you must not fritter away.' (And *he* must not go too far with his little homily.) 'Anyway, it's just an idea,' he added lightly. 'Will you think about it, Magnus?'

Magnus scuffled his feet and then made a great concession. 'I might.' It was as good as a handclasp. Well-pleased, the teacher shut down the desk, and the conversation was at an end.

Magnus ran out into the sunshine and found the Hermit digging in the back-garden, with the little white dog frisking at his heels.

'Can I help you, Mr Skinnymalink?' asked the boy.

'No!'

'Okay!'

Magnus knew how to respect a direct refusal without taking offence. The truth was, the Hermit had set himself the task of bringing order out of chaos. If he could make the wilderness blossom, it would be all his own work. No help, and no interference.

Magnus turned away and sped down to the harbour. There were plenty of other ploys waiting for him, if he wanted them. 'Come and fight,' challenged the Ferret, putting up his fists; but Magnus pushed past him. He was not in a fighting mood. Gran, too, was trying to attract his attention at the peat-stack. 'Magnus!' But he ignored the call. He would go and help her later. Right now he wanted to be alone – with old Whiskers – to think his own thoughts.

Jinty Cowan watched him go, a wistful look on her face. She bit her tongue to keep from calling out to him. At last she was beginning to learn that there was no point in trying to force her attentions on him. Play it cool. At least she had no rival – except a seal.

143